"Is this your building?"

Nathan asked the question when Lindsay stopped walking.

"Yes. See you tomorrow." She turned to leave, but Nathan stopped her with a touch on her arm.

"Are you sure you'll be able to sleep now?"

The concern in his voice brought a slight ache, more like a yearning, to her stomach. "Whether I sleep or not isn't really your concern."

"Wow. Still the same prickly Lindsay."

She wrapped her arms around her body, suddenly aware of the chill in the air. "I'm used to being independent, that's all."

"You really believe that?" Nathan gave her a long, considering look. "When we worked together on the police force, I could understand why you kept your distance. I figured you were worried that friendship would lead to something more."

"Just because we kissed that one time—"

"Hey. It was more than a kiss." When she wouldn't look at him, he added, "Even if you won't admit it."

Dear Reader,

Two years ago I took my daughter on a trip to New York City for her twentieth birthday. We had a fabulous time—how could we help it? Lorelle fell in love with the city for the first time and I renewed a longtime obsession. I decided then that the next series of books I wrote was going to be set in this most exciting of locations.

But what would the stories be about? Walking by a row of brownstones in the Upper West Side where our hotel was located, I felt inspiration strike. I could almost see the copper plaque with the words "Fox & Fisher Detective Agency" hanging next to one of the painted wooden doors.

And my main characters? Anyone who is familiar with the music and life story of Shelby Lynn will understand the inspiration behind Lindsay Fox. And Nathan, my hero? Well, he was created by me, to be the special, wonderful man that Lindsay needs in her life (even though it takes her a very long time to recognize this).

I hope you enjoy Lindsay and Nathan's adventures and that you return for *The P.I. Contest* and *Receptionist Under Cover* available in February and March 2010. I'm always happy to hear from readers so please contact me through my Web site, www.cjcarmichael.com. Stop by regularly for news about my books and to enter my surprise contests.

Happy reading!

C.J. Carmichael

Perfect Partners?
C.J. Carmichael

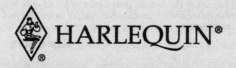

TORONTO • NEW YORK • LONDON
AMSTERDAM • PARIS • SYDNEY • HAMBURG
STOCKHOLM • ATHENS • TOKYO • MILAN • MADRID
PRAGUE • WARSAW • BUDAPEST • AUCKLAND

Recycling programs
for this product may
not exist in your area.

ISBN-13: 978-0-373-71611-1

PERFECT PARTNERS?

www.eHarlequin.com

Printed in U.S.A.

ABOUT THE AUTHOR

Hard to imagine a more glamorous life than being an accountant, isn't it? Still, C.J. Carmichael gave up the thrills of income tax forms and double entry bookkeeping when she sold her first book in 1998. She has now written more than twenty-eight novels for Harlequin and invites you to learn more about her books, see photos of her hiking exploits and enter her surprise contests at www.cjcarmichael.com.

Books by C.J. Carmichael

With love to my dad, who is dealing with an unexpected turn in the road with strength and courage.

Thanks to Barry Yzereef for entering a contest and allowing me to use his name in this story.

CHAPTER ONE

Monday morning

THROUGH THE SEMI-TRANSLUCENT glass door, Nathan Fisher could make out the silhouette of the woman who had been his partner at the Twentieth Precinct of the NYPD two years ago. Lindsay Fox had her back to him, her hands assertively posed on her hips as she spoke to someone he couldn't quite see.

When she'd packed up her desk at the precinct and cleared out her locker, he'd assumed he'd never see her again. She'd made it rather obvious that that would be best. Part of him had agreed. They were just too opposite to work well together—to do anything well together. But a lot of crap had happened since then. His life was in free fall and he no longer presumed to have all the answers.

Lindsay was smart, a woman of action, intuitive, with a keen sense of justice. These things had made her a good policewoman.

She was also impatient, thought rules applied to other people rather than her and had trouble accepting orders from her superiors.

These qualities had *not* made her a good policewoman, and Nathan supposed it wasn't much of a surprise that she'd only lasted on the job for just over a year.

But there was one thing about Lindsay that defined her above all, in his mind. That quality was integrity—something he'd seen precious little of the last while.

It was why he was standing here, less than a week after his own career with the NYPD had been terminated.

Voices on the other side of the door grew louder. Nathan realized Lindsay was turning the handle, about to exit, so he slipped out of sight, down the corridor and around a corner. He didn't want her to see him until he'd scored a proper interview first. That would make it difficult for her to not at least listen to what he had to say.

He'd spent his weekend researching her business, her new career, and he was impressed. She had more clients than she could handle, and most of them were very satisfied with her services.

Fox Investigations, as far as he could tell, was a successful going concern. This location—on the second floor of an historic brownstone on West Seventy-ninth Street—was central and convenient to the subway. After one call to the rental agency, he'd learned that Lindsay was locked into a favorable five-year lease that included expansion possibilities.

From down the hallway, he heard the door open and Lindsay call out to her receptionist, "You can reach me on my cell if it's an emergency." The door closed and the sound of her footsteps on the wooden floor receded.

Nathan waited until she was gone before retracing his steps to her office. Carefully he reached into his jacket pocket to pull out the ad he'd seen in the Saturday paper.

Help Wanted: Professional investigator. Experience necessary, references required, no attitude.

He had to smile, reading it again. Especially at the *no attitude* part. Lindsay had her nerve making that request.

He pushed open the door to Fox Investigations and took stock of the professional, almost austere furnishings. The walls were pale gray, the furniture modern, functional...and cold. The only spot of color came from the receptionist, who was wearing an expensive-looking pink blouse. She was in her twenties—a petite, dark-haired woman who was quick to smile.

"I'm sorry, but do you have an appointment? I'm afraid you just missed Lindsay."

Quite deliberately, I assure you, he thought. "That's okay. I should have called first, but I was in the area and thought I'd take a chance." He showed her the ad.

"You're here about the job?" She put a hand to her mouth. "Sorry, I shouldn't sound so surprised. Lindsay requested experience, but she wasn't really expecting... not that you're *old.* Heaven's no. It's just that we've been getting a lot of recent high school graduates, who aren't at all right for the job."

"No insult taken," he assured her.

"I'm so glad. Sometimes I wonder why Lindsay gave me *my* job. I've never been a receptionist before," she confided. "And this is just my second week."

"I think you make a fabulous receptionist." To hell with experience. Lindsay had made a smart choice, selecting someone so unguarded and warm. He glanced at the nameplate next to the computer. No matter how many gaffes Nadine Kimble made, the clients would love her. She was the perfect yang to Lindsay's yin.

"That's very nice of you to say." Nadine clicked the mouse and opened a calendar on the computer screen. "Lindsay is booking interviews for Thursday. Right now you have your choice of time slots. Any preferences?"

"The earlier, the better." Lindsay was a night owl. Best to catch her when her instincts were at their dullest.

"How is nine o'clock?" Nadine's fine, dark brows rose in consternation. "I'm sorry but Lindsay doesn't come into the office any earlier."

"Nine is good."

She studied him apprehensively, then seemed to come to a decision. "I should warn you. Lindsay can be a little…prickly. That's why she put that stuff about 'no attitude' in the ad. She said we might as well weed out the wimps from the start." Her gaze swept over him. "But I'm guessing you're not one of those."

"I'd like to think not." He glanced around the offices one more time, trying to get a feel for the place. Trust Lindsay to keep the decorating elements to a bare minimum. She always had been all about the work.

Nadine seemed to sense that he was judging the place and finding it lacking. "Almost surgical, isn't it? I'm trying to talk Lindsay into some plants. She's agreed to silk, because they're low maintenance, but I'm holding firm on real, growing plants."

Good luck with that, he thought. Obstinacy was another of Lindsay's stronger traits.

"Well, thanks for your help. I guess I'll see you Thursday morning." As he was about to leave, Nadine waved her hand anxiously.

"Oh, I forgot to ask your name." She smiled sheepishly. "I told you I was new at this."

He'd been hoping to capitalize on her inexperience, and leave without needing to resort to subterfuge, but now that he'd been asked, he gave her his second name and his mother's maiden name. He had no doubt Lindsay wouldn't let him in the front door if he was honest about his identity.

And he wanted in that front door.

He needed to keep a roof over his sister and nephew's head someway. And his father's legacy demanded redemption.

Thursday morning

WHEN SHE'D STARTED HER OWN investigative agency, Lindsay Fox had been tempted to combine her office and living space in the same building. Her sister, Meg, had talked her out of that plan.

"You need to make an attempt to separate your work from your private life," she'd argued, and so Lindsay had acquiesced and rented a one bedroom in a different building...but on the same block.

She figured she had to have one of the easiest commutes in Manhattan, which came in very handy on the mornings when she was off to a slow start—like today.

She'd had another tough night. This was nothing new for a chronic insomniac, but that didn't make the lack of sleep any easier to deal with. As long as she had time for a cup of coffee before her first appointment of the day, though, she'd be okay.

Heels clicking on the sidewalk, Lindsay took long strides toward her destination. The hazy sky and cool temperatures didn't bother her—in truth, she hardly noticed that the sunshine and warmth of summer had faded. Today she was hoping to hire a new employee and she had ambivalent feelings about that. She was glad her business was thriving and growing…but she was also concerned about finding the right person for the job. Nadine had been a bit of a risk but she was working out surprisingly well. Could she be so lucky a second time?

Lindsay crossed from the north side of the street to the south. She passed a middle-aged couple who had stopped on the corner to kiss goodbye. As she squeezed past them amid a crowd of other pedestrians, the couple separated and headed in opposite directions. Lindsay turned to the brown brick building on her left, then went up a short flight of stairs to the front door.

Inside was a foyer with a bank of mailboxes on one wall and an elevator on another. Lindsay bypassed both and took the stairs. One flight up and she was in the short corridor that led to Fox Investigations. As soon as she stepped inside, she headed for the coffee station. Nadine was already there, filling a cup for her.

"Thanks, Nadine. That smells wonderful." Her well-groomed receptionist was wearing a sea-green cashmere sweater and gray trousers, neither of which Lindsay recalled seeing before. This was her third week, and so far she had yet to repeat one outfit.

"How many interviews do we have lined up?" Lindsay asked.

"Um…let me check. I have the schedule here somewhere…"

As Nadine fussed with the computer programs that were still relatively new to her, Lindsay added cream and sugar to her coffee. Today she craved the caffeine even more than ever. Perhaps it was because of the chill in the fall morning. Or maybe it was the light pounding behind her ears. Not a hangover, quite, but close.

"Three interviews," Nadine said finally.

"Only three?"

"Maybe it was that bit about 'no attitude.' Possibly some people found that a little intimidating."

"If they did, then they don't belong here." Damn it, though, she did need to hire someone. And fast. Nadine was making inroads on the backlog of administrative tasks, but if she didn't get a new investigator soon, she'd be forced to turn away clients.

She'd never expected her business to do so well, so quickly. Just two years she'd been operating and the cases kept coming, most of them referred from her sister's legal firm, or from her contacts on the police force. Lindsay was determined not to drop the ball on a single case.

"Stanley Hodges is your first applicant and he'll be here at nine o'clock," Nadine said.

That gave her just ten minutes. Could she clear her brain-fog by then? She gulped more coffee. "Fine. Send him in when he arrives."

She retreated to her office with her usual sense of pride and ownership. This was *her* business. She'd started it from nothing and it was actually thriving. Over the past few weeks Nadine had let her know that she found the decor rather severe. But Lindsay had chosen everything for its functionality. She loved the furniture's straight lines and the tranquility of the gray color scheme.

Her own desk was glass and stainless steel. She

wheeled up her chair and opened the slick, iMac computer to find her favorite news site. Kicking off her shoes, she scanned the local headlines. She'd just relax with her coffee and prepare her thoughts before—

A timid tap on her door interrupted her. She frowned. "Yes?"

Nadine opened the door with an apologetic smile. "Stanley Hodges is here. He's early, but you said—"

"That's fine." Lindsay tamped down her annoyance as she glanced up from the computer screen. "Send him—"

Her throat closed as her mind disconnected from the present and rewound to the past. To the one, frustrating year she'd spent as a member of the New York Police Department.

The man entering her office was lean and muscular, with whiskey-colored hair and eyes a shade lighter than that. Two years ago she'd thought she'd said goodbye to him forever.

"Hey, partner. It's been a while."

For a wild moment her stomach dropped and her pulse quickened. Her ex-partner was looking good, but then he always had—if you liked the clean-cut type. Beyond his boy-next-door looks, however, the polite facade, the pressed khakis and button-down blue shirt, Nathan Fisher was a man with lightning reflexes, who kept his body in top physical condition.

For one year they'd spent pretty much all their working hours together. Since she'd quit the force, they hadn't crossed paths once, by mutual preference.

So what was he doing here now? She gave herself a moment to regain her equilibrium. Calmly she rearranged the papers in front of her, then finally cleared her throat. "*Stanley Hodges,* I presume?"

One side of his mouth curved up. The cheeky bastard. He didn't even apologize, just dropped a clipping onto her desk.

It was her ad from the newspaper.

"Is this some sort of joke?" Maybe the guys at the precinct had put him up to this. They'd all have a good chuckle at her expense later, over lunch.

But Nathan shook his head. "I quit the force. My last day was Friday, October 9, to be precise."

"What? Why?" This just got stranger and stranger.

"Let's just say I needed a change."

"I don't believe it."

His eyes darkened. "You're not the only one."

This had to be bullshit. But maybe she should play along a little. "Okay. Say it's true. What are you doing here? You can't expect me to believe that you want to work for me."

"I don't want to work for you," he agreed.

"Then—?"

"I want to be your partner."

A four-letter expletive exploded from her mouth.

He wasn't fazed. "Fisher and Fox Investigations. Sounds good, right?"

"Get out of here." She pointed at the door. Yeah, right, Fisher and Fox. He was definitely yanking her chain.

"I'm serious, Lindsay. From past experience, you know our skills are complementary."

She remembered one dark, rainy night, when it had been more than their skills that had been complementary. Hell. Why was she thinking about that? She had to get him out of here. Fast.

"When we were partners, you drove me crazy."

"You may not always appreciate my style, but you need someone like me around. Bending the rules now and then is one thing, but you don't bend them. You bulldoze them." He scooped something from the floor, surprising her when he surfaced with her red pump.

"High heels with your jeans?" He cocked his head assessingly. "Never saw you as the type."

She snatched the shoe from his hand. She'd bought the Jimmy Choo heels full price, with the last paycheck she'd received from the police department, and she was going to wear them until the three-inch heels were worn down to the ground.

"Either you've changed, or I didn't know you as well as I thought."

"It's not a big deal. I happen to like nice shoes."

"Not enough to wear them, apparently."

She slipped the shoe onto her foot, then fumbled for the mate. "Every morning when I put on a pair of heels, I'm reminded that I don't work for a big organization anymore. There is no chain of command. The buck stops with me." She lifted her chin. "It's a good feeling."

Nathan nodded. "I respect that. In fact, I respect a lot of things about you. That's why I'm here."

Despite herself, she felt flattered. Hearing Nathan say that he respected her…well, that was something.

Leaving the force had not been an easy decision. As a kid she'd wanted so badly to become a policewoman. After graduating from college and moving to New York City, her goal had been to work for the famous—and sometimes infamous—NYPD. But when she'd finally finished the education and training necessary to entitle her to wear the dark blue uniform, she'd been bitterly disappointed at the reality.

Rather than helping people, she pushed pencils. Investigating a crime as a member of a police force was like wading through waist-deep muck. Regulations and procedures ate away most of her available work hours. She'd wanted to serve her community, to protect society's weakest members. Instead, criminals thumbed their noses at her and the system as they got away with the same misdemeanors and petty crimes over and over and over.

And then there were the crimes that weren't so petty...

"You and I want the same thing, Fox. Together we'll be a force to reckon with." He planted his hands on her desk and leaned forward. She caught a whiff of his soap, noticed the clean-blunt lines of his fingernails.

He was serious. The realization sent a zap of adrenaline through her bloodstream. She couldn't help but be intrigued, even though she knew it was a bad idea.

"Why not start a firm of your own? Why partner up with me?"

"Starting a business takes time. You've got everything in place here. Plus, you've already made a name for yourself. I saw the story in the *Daily* last month. Impressive."

She knew the case he was talking about. The Anderson file had started out as a simple missing-persons case. She'd been asked to locate a long-lost uncle who'd been a beneficiary in a multimillion dollar family estate.

She'd ended up finding Curtis Anderson, a convicted sex offender on the FBI's Most Wanted List.

What a buzz that had been. Who knew how many children's lives would be safer now that Anderson was no longer on the prowl. Talk about job satisfaction.

"You've got more cases than you can handle," Nathan continued. "A good reputation and an ideal location with an excellent long-term lease."

She couldn't believe how much he knew about her operation. But then Nathan had always been the sort of investigator who did his homework. He was never tempted to cut corners, the way she sometimes did.

Her instincts were good. Very rarely wrong. Still, occasionally, she had to admit, she'd been burned by her impetuousness. In the past, Nathan had saved her butt more than a few times. He'd also driven her nuts.

"You know I prefer to work alone."

"You're the one who put an ad in the paper. Besides, we don't have to handle the same cases. We could work independently."

Much as she hated to admit it, he was wearing her down. "I've put a lot of time and money into this business. Why should you just walk in and reap the benefits?"

"I'm prepared to buy my way in."

"Promissory notes?"

"Cold, hard cash."

She thought of all the things she could buy with an infusion of capital. The extra computer programs, a new camera—maybe even a van.

Then she imagined having to vet every decision with another person. Discuss approaches, divvy up new cases. She wrinkled her nose. "I like being the boss. You want in as an employee, that's cool. But partnership is not an option."

She waited for him to stalk out the door, certain that he would. But he just smiled. Slow and confident. Then he placed an envelope on her desk.

"I have more to contribute than money. Read that, Fox. Then let me know if you change your mind."

CHAPTER TWO

LINDSAY WAITED FOR NATHAN to leave her office. Only once the door was firmly closed between them did she touch the manila envelope he'd left on her desk. Using a letter opener, she slit the top open and peered inside.

She'd almost expected to find the cold, hard cash he'd promised her.

Instead out slid a package of case notes. She flipped through the pages. Did he really expect to sway her with this?

The client's name was Celia Burchard. Burchard. That sounded familiar. Lindsay leaned back in her chair, propped her feet on an overturned wastepaper basket and settled in to read.

Apparently Celia Burchard was looking to retain an investigator to assist in the defense of her mother who had been charged with the attempted murder of her husband.

Lindsay realized then where she'd heard the name before. The story had been all over the news media for most of August.

The case had caught Lindsay's attention because of the twist on the abused-wife scenario. For once it wasn't the husband who had attacked his wife, but the other way around.

The news quotient had been upped by the Burchards' social status. Maurice Burchard was well-known as a Manhattan property developer and his wife was active in the arts community. The couple had a reputation for hosting amazing parties. To be invited to an event at the Burchards' town house in the city, or their hunting lodge in the Catskills was the pinnacle of social success.

In some circles, anyway.

How had Nathan landed a client like this?

She turned a page, dismayed to see that her hand was shaking. Just a little, but the slight tremor was enough to worry her.

Aftershocks from Nathan Fisher's visit?

She'd never imagined that she would see him again—she'd been pretty blunt when they'd said their goodbyes two years ago. Not that she'd meant what she'd said, but she'd thought a clean break would be the best—they usually were.

And now he wanted to be her partner again. What was up with that?

She knew that during their year together she'd driven him as crazy as he had driven her. He thought she was impulsive, relied on her intuition too much, didn't follow the rules.

Yet, they had had their moments of brilliance, despite the clashing, or maybe *because* of the clashing. If she could put up with their different investigating styles, the possibilities were intriguing.

Nathan was a stickler for rules and procedures, but he had other, more impressive qualities. His work ethic, for one. His integrity for another. He was also smart, a wizard at gathering background research and meticulous about gathering facts and operating according to a defined plan.

Those qualities had made him a much better police officer than she had been. Which begged the biggest question of all.

Why had he quit the force?

He'd avoided the question when she'd asked. But it wouldn't be difficult to find out the answer.

Lindsay called a friend who'd gone through basic training with her. Kate Cooper was still at the Twenti-eth Precinct, connected enough to give her the answers she wanted.

Kate answered the phone with a clipped "Cooper here," then whistled when she found out who was on the line. "Fox—nice work on the Anderson case. I meant to call when I saw your name in the paper. Pretty impressive bringing down a piece of scum like that."

"It felt good," Lindsay admitted. "You want to give this kind of work a try? Quit the force and I'll make room for you."

Kate just laughed. "Got to admit I'm tempted. But do you have a health plan? Guaranteed pension?"

"What do you care about those things? You're young and healthy."

"Thank God, yes. But when it comes time to start a family…"

It was hard to think of coolheaded, tough Kate as a mother. "Have you met someone?"

"Not really met. More like reconnected. Remember Conner Lowery?"

"Sure." Lowery was a detective at the NYPD and their paths had crossed a few times during her year at the precinct. He had Irish good looks and an easygoing temperament. Lindsay remembered him as competent and hardworking, though very charming.

"We've just moved in together."

"Well…that's great. I'm happy for you." She tried to make it sound as if she really meant it, but commitment was something she ran from in her own life, so it took a leap of imagination to consider this good news.

"Thanks. We should get together for lunch or coffee. But right now I'm super busy—"

Lindsay could tell she was about to hang up. "One second. I have something else. A question. It's about Nathan Fisher. Did he really quit?"

"You're kidding, right? Everyone in the precinct— hell, in the city—knows about Nathan. It was so unfair what happened to him."

"What?" Lindsay sat upright, her muscles tensing. "Tell me everything."

"I can't believe you haven't heard about this. It's been in all the papers."

"I've been busy. I must have missed it."

"Well, then. This story goes back several months. Nathan was on the street, busting up a drug deal and making an arrest when the perp pulled out a gun. Shots were exchanged, both guys were injured."

This was sounding familiar. She had heard something about the story, but had never seen a name or a photograph. "That was *Nathan?*"

"Yeah. The punk shot him two times in the leg. Fortunately the wounds were minor. He could have been back at work within a few weeks. But the kid's injuries were more serious and he happened to be the son of a high-powered attorney who made a huge stink, insisting his kid was innocent, that Nathan fired first, etc., etc...."

Lindsay felt the familiar burn of injustice. "Innocent, huh? So why was he packing a gun? Why did he resist arrest?"

"Exactly. Ask me, the punk is lucky not to be dead. And you know Nathan...he followed procedure to the nth degree. Still, Internal Affairs got all sticky during their investigation. At one point they even laid charges against him. Nathan was sidelined for several months and not one of the big brass said a word in his defense."

"No balls," Lindsay said with contempt. "God, one of their men takes bullets and still has to defend firing in return? It's crazy."

"Charges were dropped eventually, but Nathan was put through the wringer. Just last week his name was finally cleared. The next day, he handed in his resignation."

"Good for him." Lindsay felt like cheering.

"Yeah, who could blame him, right?"

"Hell. I can't believe I didn't know that was him."

She was just too damn busy. And right now she couldn't think of anyone she'd rather share office space with than the woman she was talking to. "Are you sure you aren't ready for a change in careers?"

Kate laughed. "Call me back when you can offer a full benefit package."

"Well, thanks for the info, anyway. And good luck with Conner." Lindsay replaced the phone, then stared at the file on her desk, not really seeing it, but instead remembering Nathan's expression when he'd told her he'd left the force. He'd been calm, impassive, but now she knew that had all been an act. It had to have been.

Unlike her, Nathan had loved being a member of the NYPD. He'd been a natural at the job, clearly a superstar destined to go far. Until he'd had the bad luck to try and arrest a spoiled rich kid with an influential father.

She couldn't imagine how bitter he must feel at having his career sidelined so unjustly. And it was so like him not to have said a word about this during their meeting. Or maybe he'd assumed she would have heard.

Lindsay made a note to start reading the newspaper more regularly.

MANY HOURS LATER, LINDSAY swirled the ice in her paralyzer and tried to believe it was a coincidence that Nathan Fisher had just walked into her local bar.

He was wearing dark jeans and a cream-colored pullover sweater, thick enough to keep a fisherman warm on a cold day at sea. As she watched, he brushed a hand through his hair, creating a stylish, messy look. Had he done that on purpose? He was scanning the crowd, searching for someone—she didn't need to guess who.

She shrunk into the corner of her booth seat at the back of the Stool Pigeon. This was going to be tough. She had better prepare herself.

Since Kate had explained the story behind Nathan's departure from the NYPD, she'd been battling the urge to call him and offer him the job.

Despite his "by-the-book" mentality, Nathan was an excellent investigator and quick on his feet, too. She'd be lucky to have him on her team, the only hitch being that she wasn't willing to take him—or anyone—on as partner.

Lindsay took a sip of her drink, then lifted her head for a second look. The pub was about half-full tonight. Several men were seated at the bar. The booth across from hers was empty, but an elderly couple sat in the booth ahead of that one. Four tables were lined up along the front window. A group of twentysomethings had pulled two of the tables together. They were mostly guys, with a couple of dolled-up girls along as sidekicks.

Though she didn't know all their names, Lindsay recognized most of the faces. The local joint was tired, and small, but the clientele was loyal.

Or perhaps, like her, they simply lived nearby. It was nice not to worry about hailing a cab when you were finished drinking for the night.

"Cute place. I like the ambiance."

Lindsay sighed with resignation as Nathan slid into the bench seat opposite from her. From their days of working together, she knew Nathan was into health food, a borderline vegetarian. This was the last sort of establishment he would choose to visit.

Of course he wasn't here for the food.

The guy had *definitely* done his research if he knew enough to find her here. That fact alone was enough to make her want to hire him.

"What did you have for dinner?" His gaze dropped to the dish she'd pushed aside a few minutes ago. "It must have been delicious. That plate is almost clean enough to put back on the shelf."

"Chicken potpie. You wouldn't like it. It's about a thousand calories, most of them saturated fat."

Nathan flagged the server. "I'll have what she had. Plus a mineral water if you have any."

Wendy Pigeon, who co-owned the place with her husband, Mark, looked at him in disbelief, then back at Lindsay. "You have a date?"

"Definitely not. Nathan used to work with me when I was a cop. Don't bother remembering his name. He won't be back."

Wendy removed Lindsay's empty dish and replaced it with a slice of coconut cream pie. "Want another paralyzer?"

Lindsay took the last slurp from her glass, then nodded.

Once Wendy had returned to the kitchen, Nathan said, "You still drink those things?"

"Why not? They're a great source of calcium."

"If you want calcium, you should try soy milk. Those things are loaded with alcohol, sugar, fat and caffeine."

She smirked. "That's why I love them."

He shook his head. "The way you eat amazes me, Fox."

"Whatever." She shrugged and proceeded to enjoy her first taste of pie. At least she tried.

Nathan was looking at her steadily, his arms folded on the table, his body leaning forward. Close up like this, she couldn't help but be aware of his broad shoulders and solid muscles.

"We worked together for a year and I still don't know anything about your personal life." The power in his gaze lessened, was replaced with curiosity. "You never talked about family or friends. Never mentioned a boyfriend—ex, or otherwise."

"I'm not much for chitchat. Especially at work." She took another bite of the pie, trying again to appreciate the rich flavor and creamy texture.

"No. Clearly you have your friends for that."

She grimaced at his reference to the fact that she'd been eating—worse yet, drinking—alone. "Hey, these people are my friends. Wendy and Mark." She waved her pastry- and custard-covered fork in the direction of the bar. "Those losers watching the baseball game."

"Right. Bosom buddies, I can tell." He leaned into his seat and shook his head at her. "So how were the rest of the job interviews? Did you hire anyone?"

She considered lying. But he'd find out soon enough. "No," she admitted. "But we're running the ad again this week. I'm sure someone suitable will turn up."

At least she could hope. She'd tried so hard to find potential in the two other applicants she'd met this afternoon. But one had been a disorganized mess, the other curt to the point of rudeness. Even good-hearted Nadine had agreed that neither one of them could possibly work.

"How about a one-month trial period?" Nathan suggested. "If either one of us isn't happy, we'll call it a learning experience and move on."

It was a tempting offer. "You still talking about a partnership?"

"Of course."

She shook her head, reluctantly. "I've gotten used to working on my own." She took the last bite of pie, then dug into her leather bag for the envelope he'd given her earlier. "You might as well take this back."

"The case didn't interest you?"

"Hell, yes, it interested me. But it's yours. I have no idea how you landed such a plum assignment, but with contacts like yours, why do you need me? You can set up your own business simply enough."

"I'm not interested in working alone. You're already established and I think our skills are complementary. Why not team up and make the most of them?"

He was making a strong case, but so far neither one of them had mentioned the other reason partnering up again might not be such a great idea. She studied the depths of his warm, brown eyes, and wondered if he'd forgotten about that night.

If he had, it was probably for the best.

"Why didn't you tell me the real reason you left the force?"

His eyes became guarded, and his mouth tightened. "I figured you'd have read the papers."

"I don't make it past the front page very often. But I happened to be talking to Kate Cooper today and she filled me in. Those hypocrites. I can't believe they hung you out to dry."

"Politics. Lieutenant Rock said not to take it personally." His laugh was short, and hard.

"And what did *you* say to that?"

"What do you think? I don't often lose my cool—"

"I'll say."

He raised his eyebrows at the interruption. "But that day I did." He allowed a small smile. "Felt damn good, too."

"Maybe you're human after all, Fisher."

Wendy came out of the kitchen with a potpie for Nathan. She always wore her dark hair tied back, but one strand usually defied orders and needed to be tucked behind her ear at periodic intervals. Wendy did this now as she hesitated at their table.

"I recognize you," Wendy said. "Your picture was in the paper. You're the cop who shot that rich lawyer's kid."

Resignation, pain, anger...Lindsay wasn't sure which emotion flashed over Nathan's face, in the brief instant before he was able to compose himself.

"That's me."

"The press hung you out to dry, but we weren't fooled." She glanced at Mark, who was drying glasses behind the bar, but keeping an eye on them at the same time. "That kid deserved every ounce of trouble you gave him, and then some. So how did things end up for you? You get fired?"

"No, actually, my name was cleared last week. Then I quit."

"Yeah? I didn't see anything about *that* in the paper."

"The story ran this Wednesday. A short article near the end of the section. I'm not surprised you missed it."

Lindsay was appalled. "So they tar and feather you in the headlines, then exonerate you in the back pages? That stinks."

Nathan heaved his big shoulders. "That's life in the fast lane."

"Hang on," Wendy said. "I'm bringing you another mineral water. On the house."

Lindsay smiled as she watched Wendy hurry back to the bar. "You sure won her over."

Nathan poked his dinner with his fork, then lifted his gaze. "More important—have I won *you* over?"

Lindsay hesitated. Despite her reservations, he was wearing her down. "I'll think about it," she finally allowed.

"Think fast," he said. "This is a time limited offer."

As Nathan eased the dead bolt into position, he heard his sister creep down the stairs.

"Quiet." She held a finger to her lips. "Justin finally fell asleep."

He nodded, slipped off his shoes, then made his way silently to the kitchen. Mary-Beth followed, going straight for the fridge.

"Are you hungry? I could whip up a stir-fry with the leftovers from dinner."

"I'm starving," he admitted. The chicken potpie at the dive Lindsay seemed to love had been inedible. He didn't know how she kept her great figure on such a terrible diet. "But I can make my own dinner. You sit for a minute."

"I don't mind," Mary-Beth tried to insist.

"Well, I do. I *am* the better cook, you know." It was so not true. He was trying to goad her into retaliating. Maybe even coax a smile from her weary-looking face. But his younger sister just melted into her chair and sank her arms and head to the table.

"What comes after the terrible twos? Please tell me it's the terrific threes."

"I haven't got a clue. But Justin isn't that terrible, as a rule."

"Not for you, he isn't, but lately he fights me on everything. He doesn't want the blue pajamas, he wants the red ones. He won't drink his milk, he wants apple juice." She sighed. "Sometimes I wish…"

She didn't finish, but he could guess what she was longing for. She still hadn't told him why she and her ex-husband, Logan, had broken up, but it was clear that she—and her son—missed the guy.

"So where were you out so late? Did you have a date?"

He snorted. "Right." Since the shooting he hadn't been in the mood for dating, or even hanging out with friends. Most of his buddies were on the force, anyway. And right now, all he wanted was distance from them.

"What they did to you wasn't right, but you can't be bitter, Nathan. The bullet wounds have healed…you need to let the mental wounds heal, too. Start living your life, again, having fun."

Nathan nodded, as if he agreed. But as close as he was to his sister, he'd never expect her to understand. Their dad had been a hero. A real, genuine hero. All his life, Nathan had wanted to live up to that standard. And what had happened?

His name had been maligned in the headlines of the very paper that had once lauded his father as a hero. Columns that had praised his old man for sacrificing his life to save a stranger had accused Nathan of being a bigot and a coward, shooting without cause based on the color of a kid's skin.

He pulled ingredients from the fridge and began chopping. "You're a fine one to talk about fun. When's the last time you went on a date?" His sister was a pretty woman and she'd moved out of her husband's house six months ago. It was time she started living her life again, too.

"It's different for me. I have Justin."

"He's a great kid, but you need more."

"Eventually I will," she agreed. "It's still too soon for me. Logan and I were together for six years."

So what happened? He kept his mouth shut, not

wanting to probe. He sprayed olive oil into a sauté pan and waited for it to heat.

"At least I have a job that I love," Mary-Beth continued, referring to her new teaching position at Columbia University. "Have you thought about what you want to do next?"

"I'm going to be a professional investigator. Like *Magnum P.I.*," he joked, citing the old TV series that his sister had confessed to watching late at night when she'd been breast-feeding Justin.

Finally a smile cracked his sister's face. "That sounds great, Nathan. As long as you skip the mustache."

She rose from her chair, stretched and yawned. "Early start tomorrow. I'd better get some sleep."

"G'night, sis." After she'd given him a hug, he turned back to his cooking, tossing the chopped vegetables and tofu into the hot oil.

Being treated like a criminal had definitely taken the fun out of life. Leaving the force had felt like his only option. But it had also marked the end of a lifelong dream. Since he'd been a young boy, he'd always wanted to be a cop. Now he needed another dream.

He still wanted to go after the bad guys. But from now on, he was going to pick the caliber of people he would work with.

People like Lindsay Fox.

Maybe she cut corners more than he liked, but she was bright and committed. Best of all, she wasn't out for personal glory, didn't take on cases just for some easy money. She cared about making the world a better place. She cared about justice.

Nathan added spices into the stir-fry and gave it a

final toss before sitting down at the table. Eating straight from the pan, he thought about the glimpse into Lindsay's life he'd had today.

When he'd seen her ad in the paper, he'd done his research. As well as checking out her clients and her business, he'd dug into her personal life. He knew that she was still single, that she ended most of her days at that greasy pub, knocking back several paralyzers before making her way to her apartment just one block from the office.

Though she was strikingly attractive, with pale blond hair, translucent skin and hauntingly beautiful blue eyes, she didn't date much. It seemed her socializing, if you wanted to call it that, centered around the pub he'd visited tonight.

What kind of life was that for a woman who was just thirty years old? From personal experience, he knew the woman was passionate. So why wasn't she involved with anyone?

Ghosts lay in her past, he was sure of that. If they ended up working together again—and he was pretty determined that they would—maybe he would finally find out.

A week later

BALANCING HER LEATHER CASE in one hand, and cell phone in the other, Lindsay dodged pedestrians, strollers and dogs, as she made her way down Columbus Street. She'd spent the morning on routine surveillance for an insurance claim, and was now heading back to the office, while attempting to return a call to her sister. Finally Meg's assistant patched her through.

"Lindsay?"

"Hey, Meg. Busy day. You called?"

"Yeah, I have another job for you. It's an out-of-town assignment, should take about a week. You interested in an all-expense-paid trip to Florida?"

Lindsay glanced up at the pewter-colored sky. "Florida sounds like heaven, but I'm too swamped to get away."

"I thought you were hiring an extra investigator?"

"I'm trying. My most hopeful candidate was a university grad with work experience as a waiter. Smart kid, but I just don't have the time to train someone from scratch."

She purposely didn't mention Nathan. She hadn't heard from him since that night at the pub and she was having second thoughts, and third thoughts, against working with him again.

Lindsay came to a street corner and checked for traffic before hurrying across.

"Look, I'm almost at the office," she continued. "Can I call you back later when I have time to talk?"

"I'm in court the rest of the week. How about we catch up on the weekend?"

"Sounds good." Lindsay snapped her phone shut, then rounded the corner to Seventy-ninth Street. Two minutes later she was back at the office. Nadine was typing madly, but paused to give her an update.

"The billings are on your desk to be signed, your phone messages are here—" she passed over a stack of paper "—and Nathan has moved into the office across from yours."

With phone messages in hand, Lindsay was already striding toward her office, when the last part of Nadine's statement sank in.

"Nathan has moved in?"

Nadine nodded. "Is that okay? He said it was okay."

Lindsay pivoted, then charged into what should have been an empty office. Sure enough Nathan had made himself at home behind the sleek new desk. He was on the phone, but he smiled and waved at her to come in.

"What the hell is going on here?"

He motioned for her to be quiet. "I'm almost finished."

"By all means, take your time," she muttered as she stubbed her toe on a cardboard box sitting on the floor by the empty chair meant for clients. A tan-colored leather briefcase was on the floor beside it.

"Okay. That's interesting. I'll follow up right away," Nathan promised the person on the other end of the line. Then he hung up.

He was wearing a white shirt today, emphasizing the golden tone of his skin, the rich mocha of his eyes. When he stood to greet her, the solid bulk of his thighs was clearly visible beneath the dark denim of his jeans.

"Hey, partner," he said. "I wondered when you were going to come and welcome me."

"Welcome you? Have you lost your mind?"

"I'm here for that one-month probation thing we talked about at the bar last week. If things go well—and I'm sure they will—when the month is over you'll let me buy into the business as a full-fledged partner."

"I remember *talking* about a one-month probation. But you know darned well we came to no agreement."

He shrugged. "Look, if it doesn't work we go our separate ways. Nothing lost on either side." He gave her a moment to digest that, then added, "You'd better grab some paper and a pen. We have a meeting with Celia Burchard in about five minutes."

CHAPTER THREE

LINDSAY STARED AT NATHAN good and hard, but he just smiled with the confidence of someone who knew they were holding a winning hand. She couldn't deny that she was happy to see him here. She didn't want to turn down another case like the one her sister had just offered her. Nathan was the best—if not the only—solution to her problem.

"This is pretty audacious," she finally allowed. "Bordering on insane. But okay. You have a deal."

She held out a hand and they shook on it. The second his skin touched hers, though, she was reminded of the one reason this might not be a good idea after all.

Well, it was too late for a change of heart. Nadine was at the door, introducing the new client.

Celia Burchard was an exceptionally pretty woman, in her midtwenties, dressed as if she'd just stepped off a beach in sundress and flip-flops, with only a cotton sweater to protect her from the October weather. Glossy hair spilled like honey over shoulders still tanned from the summer.

"Nathan, thank you for agreeing to help me." Her gaze slid to Lindsay. "I'm sorry, you're busy. Do you want me to wait out in the hall?"

"This is Lindsay Fox. She'll be working on your case, too. Come in." Nathan moved from behind his desk to give the woman a hug.

Immediately Lindsay could tell these two had a history. It wasn't just the hug. It was the way they looked at one another. She made a note to ask Nathan about it later. For now, she put on a professional smile of welcome.

Celia still hung back by the door. "I have to admit I'm a little nervous."

"Understandable," Nathan said. "You've been through a lot lately. Why don't we move to the conference room. You'll be more comfortable there."

Lindsay didn't know whether to be annoyed or amused. He was acting as if he'd worked here for weeks, or months.

Did he even know where the conference room was?

She waited for him to hesitate or shoot her a questioning look, but instead he headed confidently to the hall on the other side of Nadine's desk and opened the door to the left.

"Would you please bring in coffee, Nadine?" he asked, before ushering Celia inside.

Lindsay thought her receptionist might be put out at this request from someone who hadn't even been added to the payroll, yet, but she seemed only too pleased to spring to her feet and oblige. A minute later, Nadine returned with a tray of coffees and water.

She glanced around the room, and noticing the sun streaming in from the window at an uncomfortable angle, she went to adjust the blind. When Lindsay went over to help, Nadine murmured, "I'm glad you changed your mind about Nathan."

"I'm not sure I had a choice." Lindsay gave the cord

such a hard tug that the blinds crashed down to the sill. Nathan and Celia turned, startled.

"Sorry about that." Nadine left the room, and Lindsay took a seat across from Nathan and Celia, who had selected chairs next to one another.

What a cute couple they made. But if they were indeed dating, she was going to kill Nathan for not coming clean about the relationship from the beginning.

Celia glanced around, taking in the ultramodern table and steel chairs, then focusing on the black-framed photographs hanging on the steel-colored walls.

She squinted at the artwork. "Are those close-ups of paper clips?"

"Yes," Lindsay said, admiring them anew.

"Interesting. If you ever decide to go with a warmer look you should visit my mother's art gallery. I'd be happy to make some suggestions."

Ouch. Lindsay wasn't sure what hurt more. Celia's critique of her artistic taste, or Nathan's amused smile. She supposed she should be glad Nadine, at least, had left the room and wasn't here to add her own indictment.

"Should we start?" She glanced at Nathan, who nodded.

"Celia, why don't you summarize the situation so we can bring Lindsay up to speed?"

"It's all such a horrible mess, I hardly know where to begin."

Lindsay tapped her pen impatiently on her notebook. "Why don't you start with the day your mother shot your father in the butt, and we'll go from there."

Celia's eyes widened at her blunt tone. "It's not that easy, okay? You have no idea how awful it is to see my own parents on the cover of newspapers and trashy magazines. To have the world talking about my personal family business."

"I do sympathize." Far more than Celia could ever guess. "But unfortunately we have no control over the media, if that's what you're after."

"I don't expect you to stop them. I just want the truth. The police seem happy to take Dad's story at face value. They hardly investigated at all. And Mom's preliminary hearing was a joke. It's so unfair. I don't understand how Dad can let them put her through this."

"He was shot, right? Presumably that was upsetting."

"The bullet only grazed his rear end. He's fine. He should have told the police it was an accident."

"Was it?"

"It must have been."

"But your dad says it wasn't. And your mom?"

"She can't remember."

How convenient, Lindsay thought. She glanced at Nathan, who remained quiet. He seemed content for her to handle the questions for now. She turned back to Celia. "You're sure she doesn't remember?"

"Are you suggesting my mother is lying?" Affronted, Celia turned to Nathan, who covered her hand supportively.

Lindsay found this annoying. It wasn't their job to counsel distraught clients. They were *investigators*, for God's sake.

"I'm not suggesting anything," Lindsay replied levelly. "Just asking if you're sure."

"My mother *can't* remember. It isn't an act—she never lies. She's been released on bail with the condition that she receive counseling. I think the judge is hoping that her memory will eventually return. But…"

"Yes?" Nathan encouraged her.

"I don't think it will. And that worries me because she's so busy blaming herself for what happened, she isn't even trying to protect herself."

"You're not worried she might shoot your father again now that she's out on bail?" Lindsay asked.

"No! I'm telling you it was all an accident. She never intended to hurt him."

"Why doesn't your father believe that?"

"I don't *know.*" Celia turned to Nathan. "Why is she being so mean?"

Lindsay glanced at Nathan, reacting to his quickly truncated smile with a roll of her eyes. If he wanted to coddle this woman, that was his business. She had little patience for emotionally needy clients.

"Let's start at the beginning," Nathan suggested, gently easing his hand away from Celia's. "The morning of August 18. It was shortly after breakfast. Your parents were alone at their lodge in the Catskills when your father told your mom he wanted a divorce. I know it's painful, Celia, but can you describe what happened next?"

"I only know what Dad has told us. They argued and, according to him, Mom picked up the shotgun he uses for hunting pheasants and started threatening him."

"The gun was just sitting there?" Lindsay asked.

"Apparently Dad had been planning a hunting expedition for later that day and he'd had his gun out of the cabinet where it was usually locked."

"Isn't early morning the best time for hunting pheasants?" Lindsay asked.

"What does that have to do with anything?" Celia asked, turning again to Nathan for support.

He just patted her hand. "She's being thorough, Celia. That's all."

Lindsay ignored the sidebars. "Was the gun loaded?"

"Obviously, since my father was shot."

"Did your mother load it, or was it loaded when she picked it up?" Lindsay asked more specifically.

"It was loaded. I think. Anyway, it went off—accidentally. Mom sort of lost consciousness for a while and when she came to, Dad asked her to phone for help because he'd been shot. I guess there was quite a bit of blood, even though his injury was minor."

"You don't seem very upset about the fact that your father was shot."

"Well, I'm sorry it happened. But Dad wasn't the one who ended up getting arrested and being charged with a crime he didn't commit."

Lindsay could see that Celia was becoming overwrought again. She sighed and gave the woman a moment to collect herself. Celia drank some coffee and whispered something to Nathan. He said something back, his tone low and reassuring.

Where did he get the patience?

But then, Celia was an awfully pretty girl.

Finally Lindsay could wait no longer. "If your mother accepts your father's version of that day's events, why can't you?"

"I know my mother. Nathan's met her, too. Can you imagine Audrey shooting anyone?" she asked him.

"Not easily," he admitted. "But even good people make mistakes."

"Mistakes, yes, but shooting your husband?"

"These weren't normal circumstances," Lindsay reminded her. "People change when they're under duress. How long were your parents married?"

"Twenty-five years."

"That's a lot of time to have invested in a relationship. When your father told her he wanted a divorce she must have been devastated. Trust me, divorce never brings out the best in people."

"But that's something else I can't understand. My parents were happy together. Really, they were."

"Children are often the last to know about these things," Nathan pointed out gently.

"Maybe. I could probably accept that I simply wasn't aware of the problems in their relationship. But I will never be able to accept that my mother would deliberately shoot my father. She was scared of his guns. Wouldn't even touch them."

"Why isn't your mother here with you?" Lindsay wondered.

"She didn't want me to hire an investigator," Celia said. "But her lawyer thinks it's a good idea. And since I knew Nathan…"

"Right," Lindsay said. She'd already decided to take on this case, but she wanted to make sure the parameters were wide-open. "We will need to question both of your parents. Do you think they'll cooperate with us?"

"I'll make sure they do."

"Good. I think that wraps things up nicely," she said crisply.

Nathan offered to walk Celia to her car, and once they'd left, Lindsay reflected on the meeting. Celia seemed like a sweet, somewhat naive person, someone whose life had been uncomplicated until events completely beyond her control had shattered everything from the foundation up.

Celia may have found her unsympathetic during the meeting, but the truth was Lindsay had related with her more than the other woman could have ever guessed.

But Celia wasn't paying them for sympathy. She wanted the truth.

The facts of the shooting seemed incontrovertible. Though they often had visitors, Audrey and Maurice had been alone at the lodge that weekend—which was to be expected. If Maurice had planned to tell Audrey he wanted out of the marriage, he'd want privacy. Maurice couldn't very well have shot himself in the butt with a shotgun— not even a grazing shot. So Audrey must have done it.

The problem with the scenario, however, was that it didn't fit with the personalities of the people involved. Unless Celia's assessment of her parents and their troubles was all wrong.

Celia was far from an objective bystander, after all.

Finally Lindsay stood and stretched.

Damn Nathan for knowing her so well. He'd guessed she'd be intrigued by this case, and she was.

CHAPTER FOUR

NATHAN CAME BY LINDSAY'S office after seeing Celia out. She'd already started working on another case.

"You look busy."

"Try swamped." She put a hand on a stack of case files that were all of pressing importance.

"Want to pass some of those on to me?"

Lindsay selected a couple files that required a lot of research—his specialty—freeing her up for the field-work she loved. She handed them to him.

"See? Doesn't that feel better already?"

She had to admit that it did.

And then he was gone, before she had a chance to talk to him about the Burchard case, or question him about Celia.

The day was busy and she didn't see Nathan again. Fieldwork kept her occupied until after eight in the evening, and by the time she made it to the Stool Pigeon for dinner and a few wind-down drinks, she was exhausted.

Still, she didn't expect to sleep well that night. Celia Burchard's story was far different from her own, but the woman's distress had sparked memories, nonetheless.

At home, Lindsay watched reruns on TV, finally falling asleep around two in the morning. A few hours later she awoke suddenly with sadness pressing like a sandbag on her chest.

The light from the hallway provided enough illumination for her to make her way to the bathroom. Not bothering to switch on the wall sconces by the mirror, she splashed cool water over her face.

The dream was always the same. She was a child again, eight years old in a sun-filled playroom. Then she heard a woman scream. A man yell.

The scene shifts and suddenly she was standing in a different room, darker, streaks of red everywhere. At first glance it seems like paint.

Her father is in this room, too, about ten feet away. He's staring right at her, and she can't look at anything but him. Slowly understanding seeps through her. Something terrible has happened. The red stuff isn't paint.

Then she hears another scream and she wakes up.

The dream ends there, always ends there.

Once it had been a nightly occurrence. Now a month sometimes could pass without an episode, until, eventually, the dream found her again. Usually there was a trigger. Lindsay had no doubt what it was this time.

The new case, Celia Burchard's parents, there were just too many parallels.

Wearily, she sank to the cotton mat by the tub. Waves of hot air pulsed from the nearby heat register and she waited for the warmth to sink in. Over the years she'd learned not to fight the sadness that came to her in her dreams but rather to go with it. Only once she'd touched bottom was it possible to drift upward again.

With her head in her hands, she let the sorrow soak

through every fiber of her being. Once she'd felt the depths of it, the utter loss and emptiness, she summoned a different memory, a happy one.

She was six, recently enrolled in school, and she'd entered the kitchen, unexpectedly, only to find her parents were standing by the sink, kissing. They pulled apart with an embarrassed laugh when they saw her. Her mother offered her a cookie.

Long ago Lindsay had concluded that her memories of her childhood were unreliable, as a whole. But this one she knew was true and she clung to it.

Her parents had been happy, once.

Her father had loved her mother. Once.

Lindsay reached for a towel to wipe away the sweat that had accumulated on her face. Through the fabric she felt the cheekbones she'd inherited from her mother. The strong nose and firm jaw of her dad.

As Nathan had said, life went on. In one form or another.

Slowly she got back onto her feet, then went to her closet and changed into jeans and a sweater. No sense trying to sleep again, at least not until she'd sufficiently distracted herself. Work was always good for that.

On her way out of the room, she touched a finger to the photo of her mother that she kept on her bureau. Her Mom's smile calmed her, reminding her that not everything from her past had been terrible.

She grabbed her handbag from the rack by the front door, locked up, then headed down the stairs to the street. Though her neighborhood was primarily residential, it was never completely quiet, not even in the dead of night. The noise of the traffic was reassuring as she made her way down the block. A young couple, arms linked, passed by on the opposite side of the street. They were talking passionately about something, oblivious to her existence a mere twenty feet away.

She felt a touch of envy for their closeness and also curiosity. What could matter so much at two o'clock on a Thursday morning? She stopped to fish her keys from her purse, then made her way through the main door, up the stairs, to the office. She flicked on a few select lights, just enough so she wouldn't bang her shin on any of the furniture.

As she passed by Nadine's desk she noticed an African violet next to the phone. That was new. Touching one of the leaves confirmed her guess—it wasn't silk.

Nadine meant well, but real plants needed watering and fertilizer and constant attention. Sooner, rather than later, they all died—at least every plant she'd ever owned did.

Tomorrow she'd talk to Nadine and remind her of the company policy toward green stuff.

In her office Lindsay switched on the desk lamp. Light pooled on the last file she'd been working on. Paperwork wasn't a fun part of the job—that was one of the reasons she'd hired Nadine. But no receptionist was ever going to be able to take over the job of writing her reports for her.

That afternoon she'd shot some video footage for a Workers' Compensation case and now she sat down to compose the report. She turned on her computer, and while she waited for the programs to load, she reviewed the footage on her camcorder.

As she watched, she shook her head ruefully. The claimant had made this case painfully easy, as he'd actually had the audacity to drive to his local gym for a workout, clearly not hampered by the injury he claimed made it impossible for him to drive a truck.

Setting aside the camera, she started typing.

"The following investigation was conducted by Lindsay Fox, of Fox Investigations, on October 17, 2009, in New York City.

"On this date I observed Lyle P. Cuthbert leave his house at quarter to nine, driving his 2005 Ford Taurus. I followed Mr. Cuthbert to—"

A noise from the reception area stopped Lindsay cold. She froze as she heard the distinctive scrape of a lock turning in a dead bolt. Good God, someone was breaking in.

There wasn't enough time to call for help. She fumbled with her key ring, then unlocked the bottom drawer where she kept her gun. The weight of the Glock in her hand was reassuring as she quietly crept away from her desk, to stand in the dark shadows behind the door.

"Lindsay?"

"Bloody hell." It was Nathan. She let her arms fall to her sides as the adrenaline filtered out of her body.

A moment later he appeared in the doorway. His gaze went immediately to the gun. "I scared you. Sorry about that."

He was wearing black jeans and a long sleeved gray T-shirt. Combined with the day's growth on his cheeks and chin and his inscrutable eyes, he could have been auditioning for a role as a cat burglar.

"What the hell are you doing here at this hour? And how did you get in?"

"Nadine gave me a key. I work here now. Remember?"

"One month," she reminded him. "Then we reassess."

His gaze held hers. "It's going to work out."

"How can you be so confident?"

"I just am." His gaze dropped to her gun again. "Are you going to put that away? You're making me nervous."

She went to her desk and locked the gun back in the bottom drawer. Standing up, she brushed aside some hair that had fallen over her eye. She noticed Nathan watching her, his expression intent.

"You still haven't told me why you came to the office so late," she said.

"I was up with my sick nephew for a few hours, so my sister could get some rest. By the time Justin finally settled down, I wasn't tired anymore."

She remembered that he had a sister, but she'd thought she was married. "Does your sister live with you now?"

"Yeah. It's a temporary thing. She split up with her husband a few months ago. By the way, I've set up a meeting tomorrow with Audrey Burchard. That's why I'm here—to collect my notes and prepare some questions. I'm assuming you want to come to the interview?"

She was very interested in meeting Celia's mother and judging for herself whether the woman really was telling the truth about what she remembered. "What time?"

"Celia arranged for us to drop in at the town house on Park Avenue at ten in the morning."

"I'll have to do some juggling with my schedule. Want to take a cab from here?"

"That'll work."

Lindsay glanced at her watch. It was almost three. One good thing about this late night encounter with Nathan—it had put all thoughts of her nightmare out of her mind. "I think I'll head home and get a few hours' sleep."

He nodded. "I just need to grab that file. I made a copy for you, too."

"Great. I'll read it at home." Lindsay closed up her office, then met Nathan at the front door. He had two manila folders in his hand and he passed her one.

"Thanks." She was glad to see that he was still as methodical and conscientious as ever. They exited the office and she locked up behind them. Nathan followed her down the corridor and the stairs, until they were back on the street.

Nathan kept walking with her as she headed toward her apartment, even though the subway entrance was in the opposite direction.

"So what were you doing at the office so late?" he asked.

"I often work at night. I like the quiet."

"Still a night owl, huh?"

Suddenly she was reminded of one night when they'd been working late together. They'd been in an unmarked car, waiting outside an apartment building for the suspect they were tailing to make his move.

They'd been listening to the radio and talking. The music was soft and romantic and a mood had settled over her, unlike anything she'd ever experienced. She'd felt safe and warm and extremely aware of the attractive man beside her.

Until that moment, Nathan had never made an inappropriate comment or move, never given any indication that he might find her attractive, too.

But that night she'd thought she saw an admiring light in his eyes. When she held his gaze, he'd shifted subtly in her direction. She must have moved toward him, too, because the next thing she knew they were kissing.

There'd been an immediate spark between them, and soon the spark was a roaring blaze. They'd necked like teenagers, making love with their clothes on, and they might have gone even further, if Nathan hadn't noticed the suspect leaving the apartment building. With their guy on the move, the moment between them was terminated with surgical precision.

Later, they'd both acted as if it had never happened.

And, three weeks after that, Lindsay had handed in her resignation.

"Is this your building?" Nathan asked when she stopped walking.

"Yes. See you tomorrow." She turned to leave, but Nathan stopped her with a touch on her arm.

"Are you sure you'll be able to sleep now?"

The concern in his voice, brought a slight ache to her stomach. More like a yearning than a pain. "Whether I sleep, or not, isn't really your concern."

"Wow. Still, the same prickly Lindsay."

She wrapped her arms around her body, suddenly aware of the chill in the air. "I'm just used to being independent, that's all."

"You really believe that?" Nathan gave her a long, considering look, then shook his head. "When we worked together on the police force, I could understand why you kept your distance. I figured you were worried that friendship would lead to something more."

"Just because we kissed that one time—"

"Hey. It was more than a kiss." When she wouldn't look at him, he added, "Even if you won't admit it."

"That kiss was a mistake. I thought you agreed with me about that."

"Why would you think that?"

"You never mentioned anything…"

"I wanted to. You were the one who froze me out. Next thing I knew, you'd handed in your resignation. I felt guilty about that."

"Well, you shouldn't have. My resignation had nothing to do with you."

Nathan was silent for a minute. Then he nodded. "Good."

"I started my agency because I wanted to do work that was meaningful to me. But now you've got me questioning your motives for being here."

"Hey, don't flatter yourself. You're not exactly irresistible. And for the record, I take my work just as seriously as you do."

"Yes." She'd gone too far suggesting that he might have had ulterior motives for seeking her out. She ought to know better than to make too much out of one necking session.

Still, she couldn't silence the nagging feeling that this partnership—which seemed so perfect in so many ways—might turn out to be her biggest mistake.

MORNING CAME TOO EARLY. It always did for Lindsay. There were few sounds she hated more than the buzzing of her alarm clock, though Nathan Fisher's voice might become one of them.

She lifted her head from the pillow, then sank back as a familiar pain made her wince. She'd mixed herself another drink last night before going to bed. The extra alcohol had helped her sleep, but now she was paying the price.

She groped for the pain relievers she kept at the side of her bed, swallowed two, then hit the snooze button. Thirty minutes later, she was running late, but at least her head was back to a normal size.

As she dressed, she mentally reviewed her plans for the day. First up was the meeting with Audrey Burchard, but she needed to reschedule some appointments first.

The air was smoggy and humid, and Lindsay inhaled the familiar scent with resignation as she hurried out her front door. Bad air was the price you paid to live in this city, but frankly, she couldn't imagine living anywhere else. She passed at least twenty people during the short walk to her office and not one of them tried to make eye contact with her.

How great was that?

Nadine handed her a cup of fresh coffee as soon as she stepped into the office. Lindsay accepted thankfully, knocking back several sips despite the hot temperature. Nathan was in the reception room, too, waiting in the sitting area reserved for clients, reading the *New York Daily News.*

"Ready to go?" he asked her.

Lindsay remembered his annoying ability to always, always, always be on time. "I'm well aware of our meeting with Audrey Burchard, thanks, Nathan. Just give me a minute."

She passed a list of names and numbers to Nadine. "Would you reschedule these appointments for me, please?"

"You bet."

Lindsay's gaze snagged on the African violet. "When I get back, we need to talk."

"Oh." Nadine looked sheepish and slightly worried. Perhaps she'd hoped Lindsay wouldn't even notice the plant. Not that it was a big deal. Still, she had a feeling that if she didn't put a stop to it now, Nadine would fill the place with big, green, growing things that needed daily care and attention.

SITTING IN THE BACKSEAT of the cab with Nathan, Lindsay was reminded of the hours they'd spent together in their patrol car. It didn't feel as if two years had gone by since they'd last worked together. It felt like yesterday.

"Tell me about the shooting," she said. She was having trouble dealing with her anger on this. There were lots of cops she'd worked with who cut corners. Most, in fact.

But she'd been Nathan's partner for a year and she'd never seen him take the easy way once.

"I'd rather not."

So it was still a sore point with him. She glanced out the window as the taxi rounded the corner, then headed toward the Museum of Natural History. When the light changed, the driver sped past the museum into Central Park. They would cut through the park and emerge on the East Side in plenty of time for their ten-o'clock meeting.

"Does Celia still live with her parents?"

"You mean, her mother—her dad moved out after the

shooting. Yeah, she does, but if you're worried about her interfering with our interview, don't. I already suggested it was a good idea if she wasn't home when we arrive."

She gave a short nod of approval, then gave him a closer look. "So what's up with the two of you? Are you dating?"

Nathan looked annoyed. "We used to date. Not any longer."

Lindsay was hit with emotions she didn't like or understand. Mild jealousy that he and Celia had once been a couple. Relief that they no longer were.

Good Lord, what was the matter with her?

"You're not worried about your ability to be objective?"

"Hell, Lindsay, why the inquest? If I didn't think I could be impartial, I wouldn't have accepted the case."

"That's good enough for me," she said. After what he'd gone through the past few months, the last thing he needed was someone questioning his integrity. Quickly, she changed the subject. "I read the file on Mrs. Burchard last night. Thanks for pulling together all that information."

"I'm glad it helped."

"I knew Maurice Burchard was a big-time property developer, but it's interesting that Audrey also has money of her own."

"Probably more than her husband, since the economic downturn. Her father is a very successful art dealer. He owns several galleries that are operated by various family members, including Audrey and Celia. I believe they both have an ownership stake, as well."

"So whatever the divorce might have meant to Audrey, it wouldn't have threatened her financially."

"Not at all. In fact, from a monetary perspective, the divorce would be far more challenging for Maurice. I checked the property tax records today and both the town house and the Catskills lodge are in Audrey's name."

"Is she dependent on him in other ways?"

"Not that I've ever seen. She's an elegant and polite lady, but underneath the veneer, I would say she is extremely strong and determined."

Good for Audrey Burchard. But not necessarily good for her case. "In situations like this I always wonder about possible abuse, either mental or physical. You had the advantage of knowing them on a personal level. Did their relationship appear healthy?"

"Who can really tell from the outside? Healthy enough. The few occasions I saw them they seemed happy."

"It wasn't a facade?"

"Why don't you judge for yourself?"

The taxi was already gliding up to the Burchard residence on Park Avenue. Before Nathan could pull out his wallet, Lindsay covered the fare, then stepped carefully to the street, avoiding a pile of dried leaves in the gutter. Past the sidewalk, wide stone stairs led to an impressive set of chestnut doors.

Audrey met them there—a platinum-haired woman with a dynamite smile, dressed in an elegant suit of ivory silk, accented with bold silver jewelry.

"Nathan! It's so nice to see you again. Please come in. And this is your partner?"

Nathan made the appropriate introductions, then fielded questions from Audrey about his sister and nephew.

He and Audrey obviously had a warm, intimate relationship and she wondered anew about Nathan and Celia's history. If he said the relationship was over, she believed him. But how serious had it been in the first place?

Audrey Burchard led them through an ostentatious foyer to a library with a collection of nineteenth-century oil paintings and glass-fronted cases of leather-bound books.

Though this was one of the most expensive homes she'd ever been inside, Lindsay wasn't impressed until she tasted the coffee which was served by a woman in her fifties, who entered and exited the room with the discretion of a soft summer breeze.

"This is seriously good coffee."

"Thank you. It's my husband's favorite Ethiopian blend. It's ridiculously expensive."

But they hadn't come here to discuss coffee. Lindsay sat back in the sofa, and tried not to be distracted by either the fabulous wealth around her, or her silly, nagging resentment of Nathan's relationship with this woman's daughter.

Perhaps it was because she'd become used to working on her own, but Nathan's presence seemed to change everything for her. Focusing on work had never been a problem before. Now, the sound of his voice, his physical appearance, even the scent of his shampoo, were all intensely distracting.

It was damned annoying.

Lindsay trained her eyes on the woman they'd come to interview. In person Audrey Burchard exuded energy and power. Her demeanor was not just of confidence, but of one used to taking control of situations and managing outcomes. Her silver hair was very short, showcasing pretty ears and diamond studs as big as the nail on Lindsay's pinkie. Her green eyes were clear and sharply focused.

It seemed extremely unlikely that this woman was cowed by her husband, no matter how domineering or powerful he might be. This deduction was supported by Mr. Burchard's slight physical appearance which Lindsay noticed in a framed family photograph on a nearby table. The balding man probably weighed only ten pounds more than his tall, slender wife.

One of the theories Lindsay had been considering was that the shooting may have been Audrey's method of retaliating against a domineering, possibly abusive, husband. That, however, did not seem very likely anymore.

Determined to take control of the meeting before Nathan, Lindsay leaned forward, but before she could say a word, Audrey was speaking.

"Thank you so much for coming here today, but I'm afraid this is going to be a complete waste of your time."

Surprised, Lindsay looked over at Nathan who appeared equally taken aback at Audrey Burchard's announcement.

"My daughter means well, she's a sweetheart, but there's nothing either of you can do to help my situation."

"Why do you say that, Audrey?" Nathan asked gently.

"Because I shot my husband. There's simply no doubt about what I did."

CHAPTER FIVE

"OKAY. YOU SHOT YOUR HUSBAND." Lindsay restated this fact as calmly as she could. "But there were extenuating circumstances. Mitigating factors. Nothing is black-and-white in the eyes of the law."

Mrs. Burchard looked unimpressed. "What sort of factors mitigate the shooting of one's spouse?"

"Were you trying to kill him, Audrey?" Nathan asked, obviously fishing for a negative response.

"I must have been. Why else would I have fired the gun?"

Lindsay caught Nathan's eye. Audrey wasn't making this easy. She tried again. "Do you remember what you were thinking at the time?"

"No. I don't recall anything about the shooting. I remember having breakfast with Maurice, going out into the garden, Maurice asking for the divorce, arguing...and then nothing. Next thing I knew, Maurice was bleeding and yelling with pain, and I was lying on the grass with the shotgun in my hand."

Lindsay had been doubtful about the gap in Audrey's memory, but now she had to admit the woman was convincing. She glanced at Nathan and could tell that he was inclined to believe her, as well.

"Would you review all the events of that morning in detail, please?" Lindsay asked. "And would you mind if I recorded our conversation?"

Audrey shook her head wearily. "I just don't see the point."

"I'm sure you must be tired of talking about that day," Nathan said, his gaze warm and compassionate. "But will you do it once more for Celia's sake?"

At the mention of her daughter's name, Audrey relented. "Fine. For Celia, one more time." She flashed a weak smile at Lindsay. "Go ahead and record this. I don't mind. My story hasn't changed from the first time I gave my statement to the police and it won't ever change because I'm speaking the truth."

Lindsay removed the recorder from her bag, confirmed that it was working, then set it on the table between them. She didn't like recording interviews, and only did so when she suspected the conversation was going to be longer than her memory and note-taking ability could manage.

She pressed Record, then nodded at Audrey. "Let's start with the first thing you remember in the morning," she prompted.

"I slept in, waking up an hour later than my usual time of eight o'clock." She leaned forward and added, "I'm not a morning person."

Lindsay had to smile. "I can relate."

"It was the weekend and we were at our lodge in the Catskills. My husband was already in the kitchen. I remember he poured my coffee and made me toast, something he rarely did. That should have tipped me off that he had something up his sleeve. But silly me, I sat down to breakfast and chatted about this and that. Maurice didn't say much, but then he is by nature a quiet man, and again, I didn't clue in that something was wrong."

Audrey stopped, then sighed, as if she were imagining herself back, living that day. Lindsay's stomach tightened as she anticipated the events that would follow. The worst of stories always seemed to begin with this—a normal moment, in a normal life. At the time, Audrey Burchard had thought she was having an uneventful breakfast with her husband. Instead it had been the day her life would shatter.

Lindsay's job often brought her into contact with the worst moments of her clients' lives. It was a journey she had to take with them, at least mentally, in order to help them. Though it was never easy.

Audrey resumed her story. "While we were lingering over coffee, Maurice noticed that the squirrels were getting into the bird feeders again. We decided to go outside and frighten them off."

"How did you plan to do that?"

"With Maurice's shotgun. He'd taken it out of the locked cupboard because he was planning to shoot pheasants after breakfast."

"Did he often go shooting at that time of day?" Lindsay asked.

Audrey frowned. "No. He's usually up before dawn on a hunting day. But then, this wasn't a regular day. Maybe he thought it would be easier to tell his news if we were outside. At any rate, we went to the garden and Maurice fired the shotgun once. He didn't hit anything, but it did the job. The squirrels left the bird feeders alone after that."

"Then what happened to the gun?" Nathan asked.

"Maurice must have set it down. I think he must have reloaded it, too, in case the squirrel came back. But I'm not sure.

"I started talking about Celia, about my concerns regarding her love life—" Here she paused to glance at Nathan, who showed no reaction. She continued.

"Maurice interrupted me midsentence. It was clear he hadn't listened to a word I was saying. He told me he wanted a divorce. He was sorry, but he didn't love me anymore."

Lindsay's stomach twisted as she imagined how that must have felt.

"I didn't believe him at first. We'd gone on a holiday to Greece together eight months ago. We'd had a very nice time and discussed all sorts of things, including our marriage. He seemed happy, then. We were both happy."

"Did you remind him of that?"

"I did. I said, 'If you're joking, this is in terrible taste.' But he replied that it wasn't a joke, he was very sorry, but he'd decided he needed a fresh start in life."

Mrs. Burchard shook her head, as if she still couldn't believe it.

"Did he mention another woman?"

"He claimed there wasn't one. I'm not sure if that's true. I've thought of hiring someone to find out. Now, I suppose, that job will fall to the both of you."

Lindsay nodded. "Back to that day. After Maurice said he wanted a fresh start. What happened next?"

"I became extremely angry—so angry that I actually felt ill. We argued, bitterly, and—that's all I remember." Again she tossed out her hands. "I know it seems crazy, but the next thing I recall is lying on the grass. The gun was in my hands and Maurice was howling with pain and begging me to put down the gun and call 9-1-1."

"What did you do then?"

"Well, I tried to do as he asked, but I felt strange. I think I must have had some sort of episode. My psychologist thinks I was in an automatism state. What he can't explain, and what I can't, either, is how it happened."

The diagnosis Audrey named had been mentioned in some of the newspaper clippings in the file Nathan had given her. Lindsay had done some research on the Internet and was still skeptical. How convenient to claim you weren't responsible for your actions because you'd slipped into an alternate state of consciousness.

Seeing Audrey Burchard, now, though, listening to her describe what had happened, she was a little more persuaded.

"I realize how lame this sounds, and I'm sorry I don't have a better, more rational explanation. There are times in the past two months where I've questioned my own sanity, believe me."

"How much time passed from when you woke up, to the moment Maurice asked you to call 9-1-1?" Nathan asked.

"I used Maurice's cell phone to make the call. He always carries it with him. I remember the time on the display was 10:15 a.m."

"The medics arrived at 10:45 a.m.," Nathan added. "Does that seem right?"

"About thirty minutes later? Yes, I think so."

"Why do you think you had that memory gap?" Lindsay asked.

"I wish I knew."

She hated to press the older woman, who was clearly distraught, but this was important. "Have you experienced blackouts before?"

"Never."

"Were you drinking?"

"Alcohol? Of course not. It wasn't even noon."

"Any history of mental illness—personally or in your family?" Lindsay pressed.

"Not until now." Audrey tried to smile, despite the tears forming in her eyes. "Sorry." She dabbed at the corner of her eye with a white linen napkin. "I didn't think this would be so hard."

"We need as much information as we can get if we're going to help you." Lindsay turned off the recorder and slipped it back into her bag.

"I appreciate your intentions, but as I've said, there isn't anyone who can help me now. My lawyer is hoping that with a good medical defense I'll end up serving my time in a hospital rather than...well, you know." She smiled bravely, then glanced at her watch. "I'm afraid I have another appointment in half an hour. My daughter should be here to pick me up soon."

No sooner were the words spoken, than Celia arrived, breezing into the room wearing a short white skirt with a navy top cut on the diagonal to reveal one slim shoulder.

"Sorry to interrupt," Celia said, after smiling at Nathan, "but I'm here to give Mom a ride to the psychologist."

"Daily sessions are one of the conditions of my bail," Audrey admitted, rising from the sofa with a definite lack of enthusiasm.

"Are the sessions helping?" Nathan offered a hand

to Audrey, then went to say hello to Celia. Lindsay averted her gaze as they hugged.

"I don't think so." Audrey sighed. "It's very frustrating."

"You will get through this," Celia promised her mother.

"I hope so, sweetie. Wait a minute while I get my purse and then I'll be ready to leave. Will you see our guests out?"

"Sure, Mom." Once Audrey left the room, Celia turned to Lindsay. "Now that you've met her, you must understand. My mother wouldn't shoot anyone. Especially not my father."

"Audrey seems like a wonderful person. But divorce, especially when it's unexpected, as it was for your mother, can be a brutal and devastating prospect. You can't always predict how people will react."

"I know my mother."

"The facts are pretty incontrovertible. Even your mother doesn't deny what happened."

"That's because she's confused. But I'm not. I only wish that I'd been there that weekend..."

"Be glad that you weren't," Lindsay replied.

Celia frowned and Lindsay realized she'd spoken too sharply. Nathan stepped forward to cover the awkward moment, asking Celia if she had contact information for her father.

"I think it's better if I set up the meeting for you. He's not very happy that I've hired you."

Celia led them to the front door. Outside, waiting at the curb, was a yellow taxi and a black limo. Lindsay had no doubt which one of the two vehicles was intended for them. She slid into the backseat of the cab, leaving Nathan behind to say his farewells in private.

She'd expected he would take a few minutes with Celia, but he was right behind her, giving instructions to the driver to take them back to the office.

As the cab left the curb Lindsay glanced through the rear window at Celia. The young woman was staring after them, her posture slumped, the smile she'd worn bravely earlier, utterly absent now.

Her determined avoidance of the facts made Lindsay wonder if it was the daughter, and not the mother, who needed psychiatric assistance. But there was one quality about Celia that Lindsay had to admire and that was her loyalty to her mother.

NATHAN RELAXED INTO THE TAXI'S backseat, very aware of the woman sitting next to him. Working with Lindsay again had been a rush. Her energy and drive were addictive qualities and he had never been assigned a partner who could match her in either department.

He realized once more, how much he'd missed working with her—professionally speaking, of course.

Anything more, well, she'd made her opinion about that pretty clear last night. And she was right. They were no longer subject to the rules and regulations of the police force, but if they were going to forge a new partnership, on their own terms, they had to keep the focus on work.

He glanced down as her thigh brushed against his. She quickly shifted away, but the slight contact was enough to make him aware of her. When they'd worked together as police officers, Lindsay had worn regulation trousers and shirts and had always kept her lovely hair tied back.

He had to get used to this new Lindsay, who wore high heels and her hair long, framing her face. She'd replaced the old uniform with a new one—jeans worn with a T-shirt and a blazer—and the look suited her.

Work, he reminded himself.

"What was your impression of Audrey?" he asked.

Lindsay had been looking out the side window. As she turned to face him, a strand of her pale blond hair fell in her eyes and she brushed it away impatiently.

"She's an impressive woman. Not only strong and capable, but also down-to-earth and practical. Not the sort of person one imagines being susceptible to states of automatism."

"So you think she's lying?"

"That's the problem. I don't. There doesn't seem to be any rational explanation for what happened that morning."

"Which is why Celia hired us."

"More specifically you," Lindsay reminded him. She regarded him through narrowed eyes. "I'm getting the feeling your relationship with Celia was more serious than you let on."

"There *was* a relationship. But it was never serious and it ended months ago."

Lindsay took a few seconds to think that over. "Months ago, huh? About the time you had the shoot-out with the rich lawyer's kid?"

He should have known she'd put the puzzle pieces together quickly. He made no comment, but she wouldn't let the subject rest.

"I can't believe this. Celia dumped you when you

were down. Then, once your good name was restored, she came running to you for help with her little 'problem.'"

"That's a harsh way of putting it."

"Harsh—but essentially true?"

Again he made no comment.

"Nathan, there is such a thing as being too nice. Why should you help Celia after what she did?"

"You didn't read the stories that were printed about me. They made me sound like a coward and a bigot. I don't blame Celia for having doubts."

"Well, you should. Anyone who had spent one hour with you would know you're not that kind of man."

Her quick defense of him was more satisfying than it should have been. He remembered his dad telling him that it didn't matter what others thought about you. A real man knew that the hardest person to please was yourself. If you could face yourself in the mirror and know you'd done the right thing, that was enough.

Nathan had tried to hold on to the truism during the months he was under investigation, but it had been more difficult than he'd expected. He'd found himself excessively grateful to the few people who stood by him during that time.

"I didn't agree to handle this case for Celia's sake," he finally said. "Audrey's a good person."

"She seems very fond of you. I think she wishes you and her daughter would patch things up."

Hell, Lindsay was making him squirm here. She was altogether too perceptive. Shortly after he and Celia had broken up, Audrey had called him. She'd mentioned that she was disappointed, that she'd thought he was good for Celia and had hoped the relationship would last.

But she'd said something else, too. Something he'd never forget. "Audrey's one of the few people who called me when Internal Affairs was conducting their investigation. She told me to hold my head high. That the truth would eventually come out."

For some reason, Audrey Burchard had believed in him, when no one else—except his sister—had.

BACK AT THE OFFICE, LINDSAY handed her tape recorder to Nadine and asked if she would transcribe the interview later that afternoon. In the meantime, she wanted to have a few words with her.

Nadine looked as though she'd been dreading this "chat" and quickly followed her to the corner office, shutting the door, then sitting in one of the client chairs.

Lindsay settled behind her desk and kicked off her heels. One of these days she had to start wearing sensible shoes again. She glanced over her desk at Nadine, but before she could say a word, Nadine was apologizing.

"I'm sorry, Lindsay. I should have known you'd find out. I should have been honest from the start."

Oh, my Lord. Poor Nadine was really taking this missstep to heart. "That's okay, Nadine. It's just a small thing."

"You're not going to fire me?"

"Of course not." She'd originally planned to ask Nadine to get rid of the plant. But Nadine was so distraught, Lindsay decided she would offer a compromise. "You can keep the African violet as long as you promise not to buy any more plants."

Nadine blinked. "I can keep the African violet?"

"Sure."

Nadine was quiet for a long moment. Then she started to babble. "Oh. Good. You know, I saw it when I was buying office supplies. It was on sale and looking so sad and lonely. I didn't think you'd mind having just one little plant that was real."

"It's going to need water."

"I'll take care of it. I promise."

Lindsay sighed. Obviously Nadine hadn't considered holidays—times like Christmas when *no one* would be in the office. Well, she would have to learn by experience.

Nadine started to stand and Lindsay waved her back. "One other thing—Nathan tells me you gave him keys to the office."

"Was that wrong? But he's working here, right?"

"Yes, but you still should have checked with me, first. I was working late last night and he startled me. I thought it was a break-in. I actually pulled out my gun."

"Oh, Lord. I'm so sorry, Lindsay. Thank goodness you didn't shoot him. I wasn't thinking…"

"That's okay, Nadine." Lindsay was learning she needed to be careful when correcting Nadine, because the young woman took every little mistake to heart. The fact that she was so conscientious, though, was in general a very good thing.

Lindsay considered herself damn lucky that the woman she'd hired with a university degree, but absolutely no work experience, was turning out to be such a gem.

CHAPTER SIX

NATHAN HAD TO CALL CELIA in order to set up a meeting with Maurice Burchard, and that made him a little nervous. He was almost positive that Celia had hired him only because she wanted to help her mother, and not because she had a renewed interest in him romantically.

Almost positive was not quite the same as convinced, however, and so he was anxious to keep their conversation short and to the point, without being rude.

Nathan stood by the window of his new office. His view was a close-up of the building to the east. In other words—a brick wall. He dialed Celia's cell number and caught her waiting for her mom to finish her therapy session.

She promised to contact her father right away and ten minutes later he heard back from her.

The meeting was set up for tomorrow, at ten o'clock, at the Fox agency offices.

Nathan thanked Celia for her help, then cut the conversation short. When he'd first met Celia, at a charity auction supported by the police department, he'd been very drawn to her surfer-girl style of good looks and her sweet nature.

But he'd tired of her company quickly and his attraction to her had fizzled almost as fast.

Her mother was a different story. Audrey was a woman of strength and character. In that regard, she reminded him of Lindsay....

And, thinking of Lindsay, he'd better tell her about the meeting with Maurice. Nathan went out to the hall and glanced in her office door, but the room—a disorganized mess—was empty.

Nadine noticed him standing there. "She's out for the afternoon doing her teddy bear run."

"What's that?"

"Lindsay volunteers for the local women's shelter. She donates new stuffed animals for all the children— every couple of weeks the staff sends her a list with names and ages and color preferences."

"That's nice." He wasn't surprised to discover that Lindsay had a soft side. He'd seen glimpses of it when they'd worked together. Unfortunately they had often run across situations where innocent kids were victims—not just of crime, but of abuse and neglect.

Every cop dealt with these scenarios in their own way. In Lindsay's case, she'd used anger as a shield.

He was glad to discover she'd found a more productive coping mechanism.

"She can be a real sweetheart sometimes," Nadine said. "Even though she doesn't like to admit it. If you want to reach her about something, you'd better call her on her BlackBerry."

"I need to tell her about a meeting I've set up with Maurice Burchard. It's here, tomorrow at ten."

As Nadine wrote the details down on her calendar,

Nathan dialed Lindsay's number. Almost immediately he heard a ringing in her office. Following the sound, he traced it to a stack of files on the corner of her desk.

Under the files, was her BlackBerry. He showed it to Nadine.

"Oh, darn. She'll be annoyed when she realizes she forgot that."

"I'll take it to her. Do you know where she went to buy those teddy bears?"

"The store is called Wonderland and it's on Columbus. Only a few blocks from here. I know Lindsay would really appreciate having her phone if you're sure you don't mind. I'd go, but I really shouldn't leave during office hours."

"It's not a problem," he assured her. He grabbed his jacket, locked up his files, then hurried out to catch Lindsay before she'd finished her shopping.

Nadine's directions were accurate and he found the toy store on the west side of Columbus. The whimsical window display was geared to entice any passing child—and probably most adults, too.

A bell tinkled as he opened the door, and right away he spotted Lindsay standing by a display of stuffed animals. She seemed to be debating the merits of one plush toy over another.

"I like the fox," he said, coming up from behind her.

She started. Then sighed. "How did you find me here?"

"Nadine. Here. I thought you'd want this." He handed her the phone.

"Thanks. I can't believe I left the office without it." She checked the display for missed calls, then slipped it into her leather bag.

"You had it buried under a pretty good sized pile of papers. I see you haven't gotten any tidier since you left the department."

"True. I keep promising myself I'll clean up my desk as soon as I solve the next case, but there always seems to be something more important to do." She selected a unicorn, a pink bunny and a classic brown bear from the display, added them to her shopping basket, then headed for the cashier.

He picked up the bear, too, and also the fox, then followed her.

He'd bet most kids who ended up at emergency shelters were used to secondhand. Their parents couldn't afford new items—especially not of the nonessential variety. But then, for a kid, who said a stuffed toy wasn't an essential?

As they left the shop with their bags of stuffed animals, he said to her, "This is a good thing you're doing."

"It's just a token, really." She shrugged. "But you do what you can do."

NATHAN MADE PLANS TO MEET Lindsay for drinks later to discuss their meeting with Maurice the next morning. He had some errands to run, then made a pit stop home for dinner, delighting his nephew with the unexpected teddy bear.

He didn't make it to the Stool Pigeon until shortly after seven. Lindsay was ensconced at the same booth as before. From what he knew of her lifestyle—the fatty diet, sleepless nights, regular drinking—she had no right to look the way she did. There wasn't a blemish on her pale skin, and her long, lean body looked strong and toned.

She was chatting with Wendy when he arrived, but her watchful blue gaze soon landed on him. As soon as they made eye contact, her expression grew guarded.

He got the message. She still wasn't sure about him and wasn't sold on this whole partnership deal.

He wasn't surprised. Lindsay was a woman of action, but when it came to her own emotions, she was reserved and cautious. It had taken him a long time to earn her respect and trust when they'd been partners and he knew it would take her a while to come around to the idea that they could work together again.

He was still kind of in shock about it, himself.

Three months ago he'd had his life mapped out. A career with the police department. Eventually, marriage and a couple of kids. It had been a simple template— not that different from the kind of life his parents had led.

Not once had he considered the possibility that he would be the focus of an Internal Affairs investigation, that he would end up quitting the force and living, not with his own wife and kids, but with his sister and nephew.

Since the shooting last spring, nothing much in his life had made sense. He was a man without a plan, making decisions based on pure instinct.

Like answering Lindsay's ad and taking on Celia Burchard as a client. Usually he mulled decisions over carefully. He hadn't done that in either one of those cases.

Time would tell if he'd done the right thing.

"I hope you ate without me." He slid into the seat across from Lindsay's, noting a plate with greasy remnants. "Mineral water, please," he said to Wendy, who nodded then moved on.

"The fish and chips were delicious. You don't know what you missed." She pulled her drink closer.

"I'm sure."

"So tell me about Celia's father."

Where to start? "He grew up in Brooklyn in a middle-class family. He managed to get a scholarship to Harvard and that was where he met Audrey. Thanks to some seed money from her father, he started a property-development business that was very successful until recently."

"Is he being hard-hit by the economic downturn?"

"The same situation as a lot of businesspeople. He overextended himself. Last year his company was worth about sixty million. A lot of that value has eroded over the past eleven months or so."

"What's he like personally?"

"He was genial enough when Celia introduced us. His passion is hunting up at the family lodge in the Catskills."

"What kind of temperament does he have? Is he the kind of guy who likes to have the upper hand?"

"What guy isn't?" The news was playing on the TV screen by the bar, and Nathan noticed a familiar face. He motioned for Lindsay to turn around and look.

"Is that Audrey Burchard?" she asked.

"I think so. Look—there's her town house."

He left the booth and Lindsay followed, joining him at the bar where they had a closer view. A local reporter had stalked Audrey Burchard as she stepped out of her car and tried to enter her home.

Her daughter was with her, and they were both wearing the clothes they'd had on earlier. Nathan suspected they'd been caught returning from Audrey's mandatory therapy session.

"Have you spoken to your husband since you were released on bail?" the young male reporter asked, shoving his microphone toward her face.

Using her purse as a shield, Audrey ignored the question and hurried up the walk. Celia unlocked the front door and hustled her mother inside. The reporter didn't seem fazed when the door shut in his face. He just turned and directed his concluding remarks to the camera.

"God, they're relentless." Lindsay's mouth twisted bitterly. "I can't stand the press. This family is going through hell. What business is that of anyone else?"

"I guess when you're charged with attempted murder, you become fair game."

"So you approve of reporters like that one?"

"*Approve* is putting it strongly." This was an emotional subject for her, obviously. He wondered why.

"There is a difference between criminal activity and people who...snap."

"You think that's what happened with Audrey?"

"It must have been a psychological breakdown of some sort. The automatism defense is a stretch. But I can't believe that she intended to shoot him, or I wouldn't be on this case."

"You really pick and choose like that?"

"I wouldn't want to help a woman who had seriously tried to murder her husband. Being able to decide which cases I work on is one of the reasons I left the police force."

He nodded. He could respect that.

They returned to the booth and Lindsay ordered another paralyzer with her dessert. Tonight it was chocolate cake. He shuddered at the volume of whipping cream that had been piled on top.

"Want to share?" Lindsay offered.

He thought she was probably mocking him, but he still declined. "You really eat like this every day?"

"What else would I eat?"

"You never cook at home? Or have dinner with your family?"

At the mention of the word *family* her body tensed. "My sister and I aren't Sunday-dinner sort of people."

She'd mentioned her sister before when they worked together. "She's a defense attorney, right?"

"That's Meg."

"What about your parents?"

Lindsay hesitated, then said, "Both are dead."

Her tone was flat, and her eyes, at first glance seemed dull and vacant. When he looked closer, though, he saw so much pain he could hardly catch his next breath.

He and his sister had lost both their parents long ago. First their dad when they were kids, then five years ago, their mother. So he knew about the wrenching pain of loss. With most people he would have expressed his sympathy, maybe asked if they'd like to talk about it.

But with Lindsay, he was at a loss. She acted so damn tough all the time. Only once had he managed to slip behind her barriers, to discover the real, passionate, caring woman within.

And he highly doubted that would happen again.

"I'm sorry about your folks," he said, finally.

"It happened a long time ago."

"When you were a child?"

She was looking at the table as she nodded. Then she lifted her gaze. "You lost your father young, too, didn't you?"

He let her change the subject. "Yeah. He was a fireman. He died saving the life of a stranger when I was twelve."

"Your father was a hero." Lindsay wasn't often impressed, but he could tell she was now. There was a wistful quality to her voice, though, that he didn't understand.

He decided to keep talking. "Mom made a scrapbook for us kids, with all the articles and commendations that our father received. She was always reminding us of his sacrifice and encouraging us to live up to his example. It was a great legacy for a kid, but there were times I wished my dad had let that stranger die so he could have gone on being my father."

"Any kid would," she said softly, letting him off the hook for being so selfish.

"Yeah, well, now I'm almost glad that he wasn't alive to see my name muddied by the very newspaper that hailed him a hero."

"He wouldn't have thought any less of you for that. Anyone who knows you, would never have believed any of those ugly stories."

She speared a piece of the cake, then looked him in the eyes again. "Life can be really hard sometimes."

"Yes." He'd told her a lot about himself, but he suspected her comment applied more to her own life than to his. He wanted her to tell him more.

But Lindsay just dug in and enjoyed her chocolate cake. And he knew there would be no more openings tonight.

CHAPTER SEVEN

AT HOME LINDSAY FOLLOWED the routine that was supposed to help her have a good night's sleep. Fifteen minutes of relaxing yoga, followed by a warm bath, then crawling into bed with soft, soothing music on a timer in the background.

She relaxed into her pillows, imagined she was floating on a cloud, hoping to drift off to sleep...

But it didn't work. Thirty minutes later, the relaxing music had faded to silence and she was still wide-awake. And the person she couldn't put out of her mind?

Damn, Nathan.

Something had happened between them tonight at the Stool Pigeon. It wasn't sexual, like when they'd made out in the patrol car. No, it was worse. They'd actually had a conversation, the intimate kind, the confiding kind, the "baring your soul to someone who really understands" kind.

Meg would say this was a good thing. Her sister was always encouraging her to open herself up and to make new friends.

But why risk it? She was a happy, successful person. She had everything she needed. Most important, every day she went to work and did her best to make the world a better place.

There was no room in the equation for "opening up" and "making new friends." The people who talked that way didn't understand that tragedies aren't things you forget. They are things you learn to grow around.

Like saplings in a forest. On its own, a sapling might grow to be tall and bushy and graceful. But put it in a forest, where it had to compete for space and light and rain, and it became extra tall and thin and scraggly.

She was like the tree that had grown up in the forest. And just because the forest had been chopped down, didn't mean she could change her shape now.

Lindsay punched her pillow. It was probably a silly analogy, but the fact remained that she had to find a way of dealing with Nathan as a partner, and keeping a certain healthy distance at the same time.

Giving up on sleep for the time being, Lindsay selected a disk from the first season DVDs for *Battlestar Galactica* and watched the episodes back-to-back, until she fell asleep just before five in the morning.

When the alarm went off an hour earlier than usual, she cursed Nathan, Celia and Maurice Burchard thoroughly as she forced her body out of bed and into the shower.

In the end she made it to the office fifteen minutes before the scheduled meeting. After a quick hi to Nadine, she went to check her e-mail.

A stuffed red fox on her keyboard brought her up short.

She'd seen this before, and she soon remembered where and when. Nathan had bought this at the toy store yesterday. She carried it out to the reception area. "Is Nathan here?"

He emerged from his office right on cue. "I see you found the new firm mascot. What do you think?"

"Fox agency." Nadine giggled. "That's cute."

"And *cute* is such a good adjective for what we do," Lindsay grumbled, setting the toy next to Nadine's African violet.

"You need to relax," Nathan advised. "Have you had any sleep? Your eyes look puffy. Maybe you should have some breakfast."

"I don't need breakfast. I need caffeine." She went to the coffee station, pulled out a clean mug, and was annoyed when her hand trembled under the weight of the full pot.

Nathan took it from her. "Allow me."

His physical presence next to her was an extra frustration. Her chest tightened as she was all too aware of the broad shoulders under his dark blue shirt, the insightful depths of his eyes, the clean shampoo smell of his thick, brown hair…why had these things never affected her when they'd been on the force together?

Well, actually, if she was being honest, they *had* affected her. One night, in particular.…

She moved away from Nathan as soon as her cup was full. "Let me know when Maurice arrives." She needed a few moments alone, first.

MAURICE BURCHARD ARRIVED twenty minutes later than the appointed time. Nadine had shown him into the boardroom and Lindsay greeted him there, recognizing the slight, balding man from the family photograph she'd seen previously at the Burchards' home.

While the man was as plain as his picture had suggested, with small features and the beginning of a paunch, he was well dressed and his gray eyes were sharp with intelligence.

"Thanks for agreeing to meet with us, Mr. Burchard."

"I wouldn't be here if my daughter hadn't practically begged me."

That was blunt. Lindsay raised her eyebrows and glanced at Nathan who was just coming in the door. He and Maurice Burchard exchanged civil greetings, with none of the warmth she'd witnessed between Audrey and Nathan.

Apparently Nathan had been more successful at winning over Celia's mother than her father.

"I'm not sure what you expect me to say," Maurice began, without preamble once they were all seated around the table. "My wife shot me. I can't tell you why. She's never been violent before, but everyone has their trigger point."

"Wait a minute," Lindsay said. "You really believe everyone is capable of violence?"

"If you threaten what matters most to them…yeah, I do. In Audrey's case that happened to be her marriage."

"Don't you mean *your* marriage?" Lindsay corrected.

"Actually, no. Marriage means something different to each party involved. Trust me when I say Audrey has no attachment to me as a person. It's the institution of our marriage—and what it means to her social standing—that's important to her."

None of this meshed with what Audrey and Celia had told them. Had both wife and daughter been deluded? Or was Maurice simply trying to make light of his decision to leave a twenty-five-year relationship?

"Your wife doesn't remember shooting you," Lindsay said.

His laugh was short and hard. "Trust me, I remember."

"Have you recovered fully from your injuries?" Nathan inquired.

"You didn't see me wince when I sat down, did you? Yeah, I recovered, but that's not the point. If I hadn't turned my back on her—I really thought she was bluffing when she pointed that gun at me—that shot might have hit my stomach or my chest. My injuries could have been much more serious. Maybe even life threatening."

"Life threatening." Lindsay pretended to ponder the phrase. "So, you believe your wife intended to kill you that morning?"

"Hell, yes. If you'd seen the fury in her eyes, you'd have thought so, too."

"Excuse me, didn't you just say you turned your back on her because you didn't think the threat was serious? But now you're saying the hatred in her eyes made you certain she was trying to kill you. Which is correct, Mr. Burchard?"

"Both are. Damn, you're worse than a lawyer at twisting words. When she first pointed the gun at me I laughed, told her not to be silly. Then I heard the shot, felt the pain. Before I hit the ground, I turned to look at her. That's when I saw the hatred in her eyes."

Quick recovery, or the truth? Lindsay wasn't sure. "At what point did your wife lose consciousness?"

"Right after she fired the gun."

"And how long was she out?"

"About fifteen minutes. When she came to, I had to beg her to telephone for medical help."

"But if her intent had been to kill you, why didn't she just shoot you again?"

"I don't know why she didn't finish me off that day. Maybe she lost her nerve. But I wouldn't be surprised if she tried it again. That's why I can't lie about what happened the way my daughter wants me to. There are some transgressions a man can't forgive."

Lindsay thought about the charming woman she and Nathan had met with yesterday. "You believe your life is still in danger? That your wife might attempt to shoot you again?"

"That's exactly what I'm saying. I realize I'm not the sympathetic figure here, since I asked for a divorce. But I don't deserve to die. And I'd rather my daughter's mother didn't turn out to be a murderer, either."

For ten more minutes Nathan and Lindsay posed questions to Celia's father, but he remained firm about his version of the facts.

Finally he informed them that he had another appointment waiting at his office. "There's nothing more I can tell you, anyway," he said. Even as he was leaving the room he was pulling out his cell phone, his mind already on other matters.

A moment later, he returned with a grimace. "Battery's dead. Mind if I make a couple quick calls?"

"Sure," Lindsay said. "We'll leave so you can use the phone here in private."

"Thanks."

She and Nathan went out to the hall. She shook her head with a grimace. Clearly they weren't going to find any help for Audrey's case from this man.

True to his word, Maurice was only on the line for a

couple of minutes. Once he'd left, Lindsay went back into the conference room with Nathan following.

She pressed a button and checked the call display, very aware of Nathan looking over her shoulder. Burchard had made two calls from their offices. One was to his daughter. The second was a place called the Orange Tree.

"What does that sound like to you?" Nathan asked.

"Who knows…could be anything. Hang on." She dialed the number, and a minute later was being asked if she'd like to make a reservation.

So the Orange Tree was a restaurant. "My friend just made a reservation. I'd like a table for the same time."

"Are you referring to Mr. Burchard?"

"Exactly."

"So instead of two people tonight at nine o'clock, there will be three?"

Lindsay smiled with satisfaction. "Actually, no. I've just changed my mind. I'd like a table for two for eight-thirty. And I'll bet you don't hear this often, but we'd like to sit near the kitchen."

As soon as she hung up, Nathan raised his eyebrows.

"I have nothing against taking you out to dinner, but—"

"You aren't taking me to dinner. This is work."

"I gathered. But what do you hope to accomplish by watching Maurice Burchard eat his evening meal?"

"Nothing. I'm more interested in finding out who he's eating with."

"It's probably just a boring business meeting."

"My gut tells me no."

Nathan studied her eyes for a moment, and she felt

the same awareness she'd experienced earlier, when he was pouring her coffee. She tried to step away, but her back was already pressed against the credenza.

"Okay," Nathan finally said. "I'm willing to go with your gut. Especially since this place probably serves decent food."

"Are you slamming the Stool Pigeon?"

He looked amused. "I'm just saying I'm looking forward to dinner."

"You're making it sound like a date."

"Maybe it should be."

There was something new in his eyes now when he looked at her. She knew it was because of their conversation last night. Or maybe he was remembering that night in the rain when they'd kissed—more than kissed, to be honest. She struggled to stay cool and composed.

"We have work to do." She tried to slip past him, but he moved at the same time, putting them face-to-face. Rather than meet his gaze, which she found uncomfortable, she glanced at her watch and tried to recall the next item on her agenda. She needed a good reason for a fast exit.

But Nathan was between her and the door and he didn't seem to be in a rush to end this conversation.

"Lindsay, I'm enjoying working with you again. Although I'd be lying if I didn't admit that the feelings I have for you aren't all professional ones."

"Stop. Please."

"Do you ever think about that night in the patrol car—"

"No," she said quickly.

"Back then, a romantic affair was inappropriate. We both realized that. But we don't have a superior officer, anymore. There are no rules and regulations defining the nature of our relationship."

He took another step and then he touched her. Just a hand to her chin, encouraging her to lift her head. When she did, she found it impossible to look away from his eyes. They were so warm and compelling. She could feel the heat from his body. Something chemical was happening here. Like mixing blue and yellow and creating green, only in this case, a whole rainbow of colors was telescoping in front of her.

She sensed he was planning to kiss her. But his phone rang, at exactly the wrong moment. Or maybe it was the right moment. With obvious reluctance, he took a step away from her and dug the phone from his back pocket.

"Fisher."

Lindsay had no intention of listening to his call. She was already at the door before he spoke again.

"Yes. I could make it in an hour."

She couldn't help herself from giving him a curious glance. A few seconds later, he disconnected the call and his obvious discomfort only fueled her interest.

And suddenly she knew. The call had been from Celia Burchard.

CELIA HAD SUGGESTED A coffee shop for their meeting... a place they had frequented for "morning after" breakfast when they'd been dating.

Not a good choice, Nathan thought as he settled at a table for two and looked over the familiar menu. He'd arrived a few minutes early, even though he knew Celia typically ran about fifteen minutes behind schedule. Punctuality was a habit he just couldn't shake.

Celia surprised him by arriving exactly when she'd said she would. She turned heads as she entered the café, blond hair swinging about her shoulders, her tanned skin glowing against the light blue of her casual dress. As he stood to greet her, he knew half the guys in the room were envying him, yet as she leaned in for a kiss he was careful to aim for her cheek.

"Nice to see you, Celia. What's up?"

His tone was casual, almost cool, and Celia seemed taken aback. He felt less than chivalrous, but lately Celia had been giving mixed signals and he wanted to make sure she understood that their relationship now was only about business.

"Dad called me right after your meeting. He said he'd cooperated but that I shouldn't expect anything more from him. Was it awful?"

"Not so bad, but he did seem a little put out at having to talk to us. Still, he gave us his side of the story, which doesn't differ that much from your mom's version, at least as far as the shooting goes. His story about the marriage is a different matter, though."

"What do you mean?"

"He said that your mother values the marriage more for the social status it affords her, than for him."

"That is so not true. I can't believe he said that."

"Celia, how can you know for sure? Parents tend to hide their problems from their children."

"They didn't hide the times I saw them laughing together. Or playing with me on the beach. Or watching

TV snuggled on the couch. Are you telling me they were only acting?"

Nathan sighed wearily. He didn't want to destroy Celia's memories of her childhood. He wasn't even sure it mattered whether the marriage had been happy or not. The point was, for one reason or another, Maurice had decided to end it. And his wife had shot him.

A server stopped at their table and they ordered coffees. Nathan watched Celia as she elaborated on the preparation of her mocha latte, the type of milk and the degree to which she wanted it heated. Chocolate shavings and also a sprinkle of cinnamon. Her smile was sweet, her eyes sparkled. The server, who was male, responded to her easy charm and Nathan wasn't surprised when Celia's latte arrived with a complimentary biscotto on the side.

Celia picked up the long biscuit and dipped the chocolate-coated end into her drink.

"I don't know what I'd do if you weren't here to help me right now."

"I'm sure you'd manage, though I'm glad to be of help. I like your mother, and I hate to think of her spending time in…an institution. But we have to be realistic. You need to be prepared that this won't end as happily as you'd like."

"I just want Mom to have the best defense possible. And to do that I need to be sure we've uncovered all the facts. Maybe Mom and Dad seem to agree about what happened, but my mom wouldn't shoot someone on purpose. I refuse to believe it."

"Celia…"

"Just promise you'll stay on the case. Keep investigating. Try to find *something* that will help."

"We might just as easily discover something you'd rather not know."

"It's hard to imagine the situation being any worse than it already is." She touched his arm. "Thank you, Nathan. Mom told me that I'd be able to count on you. And she was right."

Nathan leaned back into his chair, uncomfortable with the warm smile Celia was giving him. His discomfort mounted when Celia's hand slid down his arm to his hand.

"Do you ever wonder if breaking up was a mistake?"

CHAPTER EIGHT

OH, NO. NATHAN PULLED AT the collar of his shirt suddenly finding the room hot and close.

"We had a lot of fun when we were together," Celia pressed.

Yes, they'd had fun. Celia was a happy, easygoing person. In the time they'd dated, he'd found her pleasant and uncomplicated.

"But you're also a good man, the kind that a woman can depend on. My mother keeps telling me how important that is."

Oh, great. He had a lot of admiration for Audrey, but he wished in this one case, she had just kept her mouth shut.

"You and I were never that serious…"

"Maybe that was our mistake."

"I'm not sure we made a mistake. What we had was good, though we both know it wasn't meant for the long haul."

She opened her mouth, but he didn't give her a chance to dispute him. "You're a lovely woman. It's not fair for me to tie you up, when your Mr. Right is out there looking for you."

"Are you still angry because I broke up with you?

You know I was upset about what happened with my parents…it didn't have anything to do with what the newspapers were saying about you."

Maybe that was true. But she'd been happy to lean on him for support until the publication of the first negative article.

But he had no interest in making her feel guilty. Even at the time he'd known she wasn't a woman he'd want around when the going got tough.

"Celia, your life is chaos right now. This isn't the time to get involved in a relationship again."

She sighed. "Maybe you're right. I used to think of my family as responsible to the point of being dull. I wish they had stayed that way."

"Life will eventually regain its balance. In the meantime you need to focus on giving your mom moral support. And Lindsay and I will focus on our investigation."

"Lindsay. How did you end up working with her?"

He explained that they had once been partners and how he had noticed her ad in the paper, and Celia seemed to accept the story at face value. She finished her cookie, then remembering an appointment with her hair dresser, left him with her cooling latte and the bill. Nathan watched her go. Long, tan legs, sun-streaked hair.

He supposed he should feel a measure of regret that he would never make love to the beautiful woman again, but all he felt was relief.

NATHAN SPENT THE REST OF HIS day on the computer and the phone, taking care of the other cases Lindsay had given him, but also finding out additional information about the Burchards.

At seven-thirty he went home to put on a suit, something bland that wouldn't attract attention. He checked his reflection in the bathroom mirror, wondering what he could do to disguise his appearance. He donned a pair of dark-framed glasses, changed the part in his hair, and counted on dim lighting to take care of the rest.

On his way out, he stuck his head into the bedroom where Mary-Beth was putting his nephew to sleep. Justin immediately started to cry.

"I guess my disguise is better than I thought. Sorry, sis."

At the sound of his uncle's familiar voice, Justin grew quiet. Mary-Beth hugged him close and shook her head at Nathan. "What's with the glasses? And the hair?"

"It's just a job. I'll catch you later." He took the subway to The Orange Tree and arrived five minutes early. True to the restaurant's name, an orange tree dominated the center of the room, the branches offering alcoves of privacy for the tables. A quick survey of the place confirmed that Maurice and his party were not yet present.

As Lindsay had requested, Nathan was directed to a table at the back of the restaurant, by a set of double doors to the kitchen. As he neared the table, he paused, startled to see a woman with long, dark hair already sitting there.

He was about to tell the maître d' that there'd been a mistake, when he recognized the woman's firmly set mouth.

Holy cow. He grinned and sat opposite her.

"I like the new look." Discreetly, he checked out the short black dress, the sleek high heels. "I like it a lot."

Besides the dark wig, Lindsay had altered her appearance with the heavy use of mascara and eyeliner. She reminded him of Uma Thurman's character in *Pulp Fiction*.

"Back off, Fisher. Remember, I have a black belt."

"Kinky. Want to try one of your moves on me?"

She put out a warning hand. "I could flatten you."

"Maybe you could." And suddenly he realized it was possible. This woman, with her issues and her complications, fascinated him more than any woman he'd ever met.

If he wasn't careful, she could sink him.

And he'd only just dragged himself up from the last knockout punch.

Nathan grabbed his water and took a long, sobering drink. Of all the women to fall for, his new partner was not the one.

He straightened his tie, then noticed Lindsay was riveted by something at the front of the restaurant. Of course, she'd taken the seat facing the entrance, leaving him to check out the action in the kitchen.

"What's going on?" he asked. "Did Burchard show up?"

"He's just arrived. With the most…incredible red-head on his arm."

Not wanting to blow their cover by turning and gawking, Nathan shifted subtly in his chair, then, under the guise of leaning closer to Lindsay, snuck a sideways look.

"Oh, my God."

"Isn't she something?"

She certainly was. Maurice's date—and clearly that was exactly what she was—was all curves and smooth skin in an emerald silk dress that played up her hair and her pouty red lips to perfection.

"And I thought *you* were the hottest woman in the room."

Something jabbed his shin. "Ouch." Those shoes of hers were lethal.

Lindsay narrowed her eyes. "I'd say she's mid-thirties. A good fifteen years younger than him." She shook her head, disgusted.

"The rich men have all the luck, huh?"

"Call me crazy but this redhead doesn't look like any businesswoman I've ever met."

He knew what she meant. Any woman could glam herself up for an evening, but this lady oozed sex appeal…the kind that usually was only available at certain after-hours clubs.

"I spent the afternoon digging up as much as I could about Maurice and his business dealings. I found lists of the people who sit on various boards with him, the top executives at his firm. In most cases there were pictures, but none of them looked anything like her."

"Where do you think she came from?"

"I wish I had a clue."

Lindsay wrinkled her nose. "She sure isn't subtle. She's all over Burchard. And he's loving it."

"Seems like they each have something the other one wants."

"She has sex and he has money," Lindsay agreed.

"A match made in New York City."

"And at Audrey Burchard's expense. According to her, their marriage was on solid footing just eight months ago."

"Until Hurricane Redhead came on the scene."

"She may have nothing to do with what happened between Maurice and Audrey the day of the shooting," Lindsay said. "Still, it would be interesting to know how long she and Burchard have been seeing one another and where she was that day."

"There are a lot of things about that woman that would be interesting to find out."

Lindsay stiffened, like a hunting dog who'd just caught a scent. "I believe the seductress is headed for the ladies' room. And would you look at that—she's carrying a black clutch, too. I believe this is my opening—"

Nathan risked another glance. Maurice was by himself at the table, his gaze following his date's progress across the room.

Meanwhile Lindsay opened her handbag, removed her identification, which she handed to Nathan, then palmed her camera.

"Wish me luck." She smiled at him, then followed their mark into the washroom.

DESPITE THE FACT THAT SHE WAS in hot pursuit of a surveillance subject, Lindsay was very aware of Nathan as she left their table. She was one hundred percent certain his eyes were on her backside as she made her way to the restroom on the other side of the restaurant.

The stretch fabric of her dress clung to her skin as she moved, and her legs felt extra long in the four-inch heels she'd chosen for the night. If she'd been smarter, she would have picked a different disguise for the evening. Something frumpy and dull.

But you didn't. So what do you suppose that means?

Was she encouraging Nathan's interest…if so, was that wise?

Setting aside the uncomfortable questions for the moment, Lindsay took a deep breath then pushed open the door to the washroom. Adrenaline hummed through her body, kicking her senses into action mode.

The room was dimly lit, thankfully, with two porcelain sinks set into a long marble countertop. Beyond the sinks were three washroom stalls, the doors louvered in a rich mahogany-colored wood.

Maurice's date was standing by one of the mirrors, checking the skin under her eyes for smudges. Her handbag was on the counter next to the sink. A quick glance at close-up range gave Lindsay a couple more facts to add to the file.

The hair was dyed, the boobs were fake and the lips had been colored over the line.

She went to the next mirror, removed her own lipstick from her purse and made a quick touch-up. The second the redhead turned to reach for a paper towel, Lindsay snatched her small black bag, leaving her own purse on the counter, and headed to a washroom stall.

Once inside she worked quickly. The redhead's purse didn't hold much. A lipstick, a tissue and a single key. In a small zipper compartment she found a folded hundred dollar bill, an American Express credit card and a business card. The name on both pieces of identification was the same: Paige Stevens.

Lindsay snapped a photograph of the cards, using the

sound of the flushing toilet to mask the click and flash of the camera.

"Excuse me?" Paige Stevens was speaking, her tone tinged with annoyance. "I believe you took my purse."

"I'm so sorry. My mistake." Lindsay emerged from the stall, shaking her head with faked consternation. With a tight smile, Paige exchanged handbags with her. She opened the small bag, checked the contents, then swung out of the ladies' room on a huff of disapproval.

Lindsay paused a moment to check her reflection. Her cheeks were splashed with color and her eyes sparkled. She couldn't hide her elation. Damn, but that had been fun.

"A SOCIAL SECURITY CARD would have been much more helpful. Even a date of birth. I could really find stuff with a date of birth."

Nathan passed the camera back to her and Lindsay tucked it safely into her purse. "We've got a hell of a lot more than we did at the beginning of the evening," she pointed out.

They were on to the dessert course now, prolonging their meal while the lovebirds gazed into one another's eyes. Anticipating the need to make a quick getaway, Nathan had already handed his credit card to their server. A moment later it was returned in a leather folder with a pen.

As Nathan signed, Lindsay said, "Save the receipt for Nadine. She'll make sure you're refunded at the end of the month."

Nathan paused. "No need. Dinner's on me. We can call this our first date."

Lindsay almost choked on the mouthful of red wine she'd just imbibed. She grabbed her napkin from her lap and covered her mouth. Once she'd recovered, she said, "We're spying on a married man and his illicit lover, I just switched handbags with said lover to get a copy of her identification, and now we're waiting for them to leave so we can follow them home. Some date."

"It may not be everyone's idea of a good time, but it works for me."

She had to laugh. One point she had to give him. He looked good enough to be on a date. Who would have guessed Nathan Fisher could wear a suit and tie with such style? The glasses were a great touch, giving him an intellectual look that actually suited his personality.

Lindsay tensed as she noticed movement from Maurice and Paige's table. "They're leaving," she whispered. "Hurry up and grab that receipt. They're almost at the door."

Nathan finished penning his signature, then rushed around to pull her chair from the table. "Couldn't you have given me a little more notice?"

"I was…distracted." She sucked in her breath as his hand settled on the curve of her lower back. Like she was going to admit she'd been ogling him.

Together they wove between tables, past the verdant orange tree and out to the street.

Her mind grew sharper in the cooler air, and she jostled for position amid the crowds of people. They were just a few blocks off Broadway and a show must have let out only minutes ago because the streets were jammed.

"This way," Nathan said, grabbing her hand.

Progress was slow, but at least they managed to move faster than the taxis and limos stalled on the roads.

"I see them," Nathan said, his mouth inches from her ear. He pointed west and then pulled Lindsay close while he muscled his way through the crowd.

She let him take the lead, because with his broad shoulders it was easier that way. After a few blocks, the traffic grew lighter. Wanting to let the other couple gain some distance, she and Nathan stopped in front of a shop window. On display were the tackiest bras, garter belts and fishnet stockings she had ever seen.

"Who wears that stuff?"

Nathan cocked his head in contemplation. "Not your style, huh?"

"Hardly." She pulled on his arm. "Okay, let's get moving. They just crossed the street and turned up Madison."

Nathan accelerated, still keeping a firm hold on her hand. "How do you move so quickly with those heels?"

"Not without pain, let me assure you." She made another mental note to herself to invest in comfortable shoes next time. The black boots she'd worn as a cop hadn't made much of a fashion statement, but she could run the hundred-yard dash in them, no problem.

They were nearing the corner when Lindsay spotted their marks again. Maurice was raising his arm in the air...

"They're hailing a cab," Nathan realized in the same instant that she did.

Lindsay made note of the black numbers on the back of their yellow cab, while Nathan stepped out to the street, practically risking his neck to grab one for them, too. Soon they were huddled together in the backseat.

"We're headed for the same place they are," Lindsay said, giving the driver the number she'd just memorized. Once they'd left midtown behind, they made better time and about twenty minutes later they were stopped a half block away from a stone-fronted apartment building on the Upper East Side, just south of the Guggenheim.

Maurice and Paige emerged from their taxi onto the street.

"Wait here a bit," Lindsay instructed the driver. She and Nathan watched as the couple went inside. About three minutes later lights went on in the windows of the penthouse apartment.

"There we have it," Nathan said in a low voice. "We've found the love nest."

Lindsay made note of the exact address and then instructed the driver to take them home.

With typical New York City disinterest, the driver didn't ask any questions. He just did as asked and turned the car in the direction of the park. A minute later the vehicle was gliding smoothly through the dark.

Lindsay was suddenly aware of Nathan's arm around her shoulders. She felt his chin brush the side of her head as he leaned even closer.

"You smell as good as you look," he told her.

"Stop the act already. We're done working for tonight." She slid to the far side of the seat, then pulled off her wig and shook out her hair.

"Damn, but these things are hot." She knew Nathan was watching as she ran her fingers through her hair, and she found that unexpectedly exciting. Pressing her lips together, she did her best to ignore the burn of attraction.

Nothing has changed, she told herself. *He was just mocking me. This isn't really a date.*

"We'll have the driver drop you off at your place first." Nathan leaned forward to give the instructions but she interrupted.

"Actually, I was planning to stop in at the office."

"Lindsay, it's eleven o'clock. What do you need to do now that you can't do in the morning?"

"A lot of things. You know I like working at night. Have the driver drop you home first, if you prefer."

"Like hell I'm going home. And we're not going to the office, either. I assume you want to find out more about this Paige Stevens. Do you have a computer at your place?"

"Of course I do."

"Let's go there, then."

She was prepared to argue, but he'd already given her address to the driver and suddenly she was just too tired. She'd been up early for the meeting with Maurice Burchard and the one good thing about going to her apartment rather than the office was that she'd be able to change out of this constricting dress and ditch the heels.

Besides, she didn't keep any alcohol at the office.

"Don't think you're going to get your way this easily all the time."

"This was easy? Girl, you kill me."

LINDSAY OPENED HER FRONT DOOR and flicked on the hall light. "Come on in," she invited Nathan. With relief, she kicked off her heels, then hung her wig on a peg of her coatrack.

She headed down the hall, turned on the kitchen light. "Do you know how to mix a paralyzer?"

"I used to be a bartender."

"Really?" She did not see him as the type, at all.

"Paid my way through college."

"Funny. That's what I did, too. Anyway, everything you'll need is in the fridge. I'm going to change. I'll be right back."

"Need help with the zipper?"

He was standing in the doorway, one hand resting on the frame, the other loosening his tie. He looked sexy, there was no other word to describe it. She turned away abruptly. "As if."

In her bedroom, though, she did struggle with the damn thing, and ended up tearing the fabric of her dress a little. She shimmied the rest of the way out of the garment, then released the hooks on her strapless bra.

"Your drink is ready," Nathan called from the kitchen.

She opened the bedroom door a crack. "I'll be right out. The computer is on the desk in the living room if you want to get started without me."

She sighed with relief as she pulled on the comfy clothes she usually wore for yoga. After giving her hair a good brushing to rid herself of the itchy feeling from wearing the wig, she joined Nathan in the living room.

He was already sitting at the desk, typing rapidly, focus intent on the screen. Nathan was an expert when it came to the computer. If there was any information to be gained about Paige Stevens on the Web, he'd find it.

Her drink was waiting on the table next to the sofa.

She settled into the cushions, then took a sip. "You didn't mix one for yourself?"

"No," he said, his tone absentminded. "I had enough wine at the restaurant."

He'd had maybe two glasses over the course of the entire evening. Lindsay knew she'd drunk more than that, and wondered if he'd kept track.

"Need any help?" she asked. "I'm feeling kind of lazy, here."

"You relax. I'll let you know if I find anything illuminating. By the way…" his fingers still clattered on the keys "…interesting photos on your fridge. Is that your sister?"

"Yes." Her stomach tightened reflexively, the way it always did when someone asked questions about her family. But she should have seen this one coming. Why didn't she keep her photos in an album, instead of tacked to the front of her refrigerator?

"What firm does she work for?"

"Livingstone and Fagan. She throws a lot of work my way. You're sure to meet her, eventually."

"I'd like that. Judging by those photos you and your sister have traveled to some exciting places."

"We're on a quest to visit all seven continents. It's our Christmas tradition."

"What about trimming the tree and turkey dinner?"

"Not our style."

He swiveled in the chair to look at her. She kept her face expressionless, and his glance fell to the empty glass on the table.

"You finished that quickly."

"Are you judging me?"

"Not at all. Just wondering if you'd like a refill."

His calm response made her suspicious. Still, when she nodded, he picked up her glass, returned to the kitchen and came back less than a minute later with a fresh drink. After setting it on the table, he returned to the computer.

"Is your printer connected?"

"Sure. What have you found?"

"The real estate office where Paige Stevens works has a Web site. Seems like her specialty is commercial real estate. She's listed as one of their top agents. I'm printing out the address and phone number."

Lindsay took a long swallow of her drink, then closed her eyes, savoring the sensation. "This is good, Fisher."

He didn't acknowledge the compliment. "Maybe Burchard met Stevens over a real estate deal."

"That sounds logical." Lindsay put up her feet and took another swallow. "Tomorrow I should pretend to be in the market for a new location for my business and see what I can learn from her coworkers. Oh, and we need to talk to her neighbors in the apartment complex. And the doorman. Maybe they can give us an idea how long this affair has been going on."

Lindsay polished off her drink and wondered if she dared ask Nathan to make her another. She'd get up and do it herself, only she was feeling really, really comfortable right now. She slid down the sofa a little, until her head was resting on one of the pillows.

"Interesting," Nathan said. "Guess who owns the love-nest apartment building?"

She was floating on a lovely cloud of dulled sensation, yet still she managed to connect the dots. "Maurice Burchard?"

"Exactly, right. He bought it about five months ago. Borrowed a lot of money to do it, too."

"What a jerk. He didn't even have the guts to come clean with his wife on why he wanted a divorce."

"It sucks for Audrey, but it's good for her case. The fact that she didn't know about the affair will make her more sympathetic to the judge and jury. We're finally getting somewhere on this case, Fox."

Those were the last words Lindsay heard as she drifted smoothly into sleep that, for once, did not elude her.

CHAPTER NINE

LINDSAY WAS SNORING. Not loud, obnoxious snoring but a gentle rumble that he found quite endearing. Nathan shut down the computer and went to check on her. She'd had a lot to drink tonight, but then it seemed she had a lot to drink every night.

She looked different with her face relaxed. Softer. Younger. He knew she wouldn't appreciate being watched like this, though—she guarded her vulnerability at all costs—and so he turned around, looking for a blanket.

Finding nothing in the living room, he checked the bedroom. Lindsay's bed was unmade. The unholy mess spoke of hours spent tossing and turning. He untangled one of the blankets and was on his way out of the room, when two photos on the bureau caught his attention.

He shouldn't snoop, he knew it was wrong, yet he couldn't resist a quick look. One photo showed a woman in her late twenties. She had Lindsay's smooth, translucent skin and the sort of big blond curls that were popular in the eighties. Figuring that this must be a picture of her mother, it followed that the photo of the man right next to it must be her father.

Here Nathan saw a man with Lindsay's pale blue

eyes—not quite as haunted as hers, but still troubled. Draped over the picture frame was an Air Force Medal of Honor—for service in the Vietnam War, he presumed.

Intrigued by this glimpse at Lindsay's heritage, Nathan returned to the living room where he gently covered her with the blanket. Resisting the urge to brush a strand of hair from her cheek, he picked up her empty glass and carried it to the kitchen. Rather than place it into a dishwasher that he suspected was rarely used, he washed the glass by hand and replaced it in the cupboard.

The photos on the fridge caught his attention again. There was a family resemblance between the sisters, but Meg's features were softer, he supposed some would say prettier. Together they had been photographed at the lip of a volcanic crater, at the top of a snow-covered mountain, standing at the prow of a sailboat and in a Jeep on safari.

In every picture, no exception, the sisters had their arms entwined, heads inclined toward one another. The closeness of their relationship was very evident.

He wondered if their decision to travel every Christmas had been made for practical reasons, or because they wanted to avoid the holiday and all it represented.

After their mother had died, Christmas had been hard for him and Mary-Beth, too. Justin's arrival had changed all that, given the holiday new meaning.

Nathan slipped the door key off the ring Lindsay had tossed on the kitchen counter. Once he'd securely locked the dead bolt, he'd slip her key back under her door.

He turned out all the lights, saving the one by the

front door for last. Just as he was pressing down on the switch, he heard a faint voice from the living room.

"Leave the hall light on, please."

"Lindsay?"

No answer. She'd fallen back asleep.

IT WAS ALMOST ONE IN THE morning when Nathan finally made it home. He was surprised to find Mary-Beth awake, watching a rerun of *Grey's Anatomy*.

"Don't tell me Justin isn't sleeping again?" He locked the door behind himself, then hung his jacket in the closet.

"No. This time I'm the one with the sleeping problem." She gave him a weary smile, then clicked off the television.

"I seem to be surrounded by insomniacs lately."

"Oh? Who else?"

"This woman I'm working with."

"Lindsay Fox?"

"That's the one."

"You get this funny look on your face whenever you talk about her. Like you're trying really hard to act like she isn't important to you."

"I work with her, so obviously she's important to me."

"Right." Mary-Beth smiled. "So why can't *she* sleep?"

"I'm guessing it has something to do with her family. She's close to her sister, but they lost their parents and it must have been traumatic. She won't talk about it."

Mary-Beth's face softened with sympathy. "Did they pass away recently? I couldn't sleep for months after Mom's accident."

"I'm not sure," he admitted. He ruffled his sister's

messy curls. "And what about you? What's your excuse?"

"I'm worried about Justin. About his future. I'm having trouble letting go of my dreams for what his life was supposed to be like. I wanted it to be storybook perfect for him, like it was for us."

"Our childhood was *not* storybook perfect. Have you forgotten what a bad cook Mom was? And those endless, boring stories Dad would tell on long car rides?" He stopped, looked at the longing expression on Mary-Beth's face, and sighed. "Actually, it came pretty damn close to perfect, didn't it?"

"We were lucky."

"We didn't know it at the time. But yeah. We were *damn* lucky. At least until the fire."

"Yes, but we were old enough to remember our father. Justin won't have those sorts of memories since work seems to be the only thing that matters to Logan."

"Is that why you two split up?"

Mary Beth pressed her lips together and nodded. "Now there's just me for my son and how can I possibly be enough?"

Before he could give her an answer, she held up her hand to stop him. "I know you plan to be in Justin's life as much as you can. And that will be wonderful. But we can't live with you forever and having an uncle won't be the same as having a dad."

"Whoa, Mary-Beth. Why assume the worst? You could still meet a great guy. Or Logan might come to his senses."

"Not likely. He phoned me today with big news. He's accepted a job transfer to London, England."

"Wow."

"Yeah. He didn't ask if we wanted to come along."

"I'm sorry, sis."

"In a way it's good. I realize I've been living in limbo the last while, afraid to make new plans in case Logan and I got back together. Now I know that we won't."

"That guy must be crazy to be walking out on you two." It was hard not to be angry, on Mary-Beth's behalf. She deserved better than this.

"Well, it's his life. Now I need to do what's right for Justin and me. I've been looking at apartments and they're very expensive."

"Hey. You don't need to move out of this one."

"It's small for two adults and a child," she said. "And you need your privacy."

"Mary-Beth—"

"Don't worry. Justin and I won't be out on the street. There's a woman I teach with—her name is June Stone. She's quite a bit older than me, very bright, a lovely woman, but she's not well. She has a lead on a rent-controlled co-op in her building. Tomorrow I'm going to take a look."

"This is really out of the blue, sis."

"I know. I haven't decided for sure, but I'm seriously thinking about it. And I wanted to tell you."

He waited to see if this time she'd fill in more blanks, but all she did was yawn.

"Maybe I'll try to sleep again. Morning comes quickly when you have a two-year-old."

"Good idea."

She started for the stairs, then looked back at him. "Are you sure you're okay? You were out late tonight."

"Surveillance," he reminded her.

"With *Lindsay?*"

He groaned. "Maybe you're right. Maybe I do need a little more privacy around here."

LINDSAY DIDN'T ENJOY the luxury of sleeping through the night very often. She stretched until her toes reached the edge of the sofa, then snuggled back into the blanket Nathan must have covered her with last night.

He'd been here in her apartment with her. Mixing her drinks. Working on her computer. Grabbing this blanket from her bedroom.

She swallowed, remembering the last words she'd called out to him. God, he must have laughed at the idea that she needed the hall light on.

Only…she didn't think he would have laughed. But he probably would have wondered. Not too many people were afraid of the dark once they'd left their childhood years behind. But that was the problem, wasn't it? She hadn't left her childhood years behind, not really. And neither had Meg.

She thought about her sister, about the eating disorders that had been linked to the trauma of their childhood and that made it so difficult for her sister to do such ordinary things as eat out at restaurants or travel. In fact, the only time she would consider taking a holiday was if Lindsay went with her.

Not that Lindsay minded spending time with her sister. She loved it. She just wished, for Meg's sake, that life could be a little easier for her.

From the bedroom came the muffled sound of her morning alarm. Lindsay allowed herself one last, delicious stretch, then left the cushioned softness of the sofa and headed for the bedroom to turn off the alarm. While she was there, she grabbed a pain reliever for the headache that was just starting to pound at the back of her skull.

The wine. The paralyzers. The sins of her evening coming back to haunt her.

She didn't care. It had been worth it to sleep through the night for a change.

You sure it wasn't Nathan tucking you in last night that had you sleeping so soundly?

Normally Lindsay paid a lot of attention to the little voice at the back of her mind. This morning, though, she ignored it.

NATHAN SPENT THE NEXT DAY on the computer, putting together a history on Paige Stevens. Lindsay was out in the field, doing the sort of work she loved—checking out the firm where Paige worked and the apartment building where Paige and Maurice had spent the night.

Just before five, Nathan took a break from the computer and went to talk to Nadine. "Heard anything from Lindsay?"

"Not a thing." She looked flustered. "And there were so many calls. How was your day? You were awfully quiet back there."

"It's amazing what you can find out about a person just from judicious use of the Internet and a few phone calls." He'd already told Nadine what he and Lindsay had discovered yesterday. She'd been appalled and intrigued, in equal measure.

Nadine checked the time, saw that it was five and got up to clean out the coffee machine. As she dumped the filter into the trash she was careful not to spill any grinds on her expensive-looking, cream-colored suit.

"I've noticed that Lindsay does a lot of background checks. And sometimes she needs to find out if someone is married, or if they've died or have a record. Is that all stuff you learn how to do during police training?"

"Some of it we learned in training. Other stuff we picked up on the job."

"What about people who've never worked for the police? Can they be professional investigators, too?"

He wondered where she was going with all these questions. "Sure."

"How?"

"I assume we're talking about you?"

She hesitated, then smiled sheepishly.

"Hey, don't be embarrassed. It's not hard to get your license as a private investigator. First, you need to apprentice with an experienced investigator. And there are courses. Some of them are offered online. Have you told Lindsay you're interested in this?"

"Me? Oh, I'm still learning the ropes at the receptionist job. I don't have a lot of practical skills, to be perfectly honest."

Her assessment of herself surprised him. "Why would you say that?"

"The way I was raised." She lowered her voice. "My family has a lot of money. I didn't tell Lindsay because I wanted this job and when people find out what my father's last name is, they never hire me. Or they hire me *because* of my father's last name and I didn't want that, either."

"But…didn't you have to tell Lindsay your last name when you filled out your application?"

"I made up a name."

He tried to hide his shock. "How do you deposit your paycheck?"

"I haven't earned one, yet. My first payday is next Friday." She bit her bottom lip. "That's going to be a problem, isn't it?"

"This is incredible, Nadine. You have to tell Lindsay the truth."

She cast her eyes down, guiltily. "I know. I was hoping to prove myself first."

"I can relate to that," Nathan said, thinking of his own arrangement with Lindsay. "She's a tough broad sometimes, but she's fair."

"Yes, besides, she can't be too upset with me. After all, she changed her last name, too."

"Lindsay did?"

Nadine nodded. "I saw the forms when I was organizing the filing cabinet. Her last name used to be Yzereef. Oh. I probably shouldn't have said that."

"Not to worry." It felt wrong to pump a sweetheart like Nadine for information, but his curiosity was so strong, he couldn't resist. "Yzereef. That's an unusual name. How do you spell it?"

She showed him. "It's hard to spell and I have no clue if I'm pronouncing it correctly. That's probably why she— Oh." Nadine glanced at the door as it opened. "Hi, Lindsay!"

LINDSAY WONDERED WHAT NADINE and Nathan had been discussing. Nadine's cheeks were pink, and her gaze slid guiltily to the left of Lindsay's face when she greeted her.

In contrast, Nathan appeared cool and slightly amused. He had his hands behind his back, leaning on Nadine's desk.

She took in these details automatically because she'd been trained to do this, it was her job and by now, her nature.

But she was too excited by the day's discoveries to be distracted for long. "I just had the most productive day. Sometimes I love my job," she added smugly.

"You love any job that doesn't entail paperwork and administrative details," Nathan observed.

"Your specialty," Lindsay pointed out. "And Nadine's."

"Speaking of which…" Nadine held out a stack of paper. "I couldn't get in touch with you all day. A few things came up."

"Sorry. I spent the morning pretending to be in the market for commercial real estate and the afternoon making friends with the doorman at an apartment building on Fifth Avenue. I didn't want to risk a call coming in at just the wrong moment so I kept my phone off."

She accepted the messages, some including case summaries that Nadine had taken over the phone. She frowned as she leafed through them. A couple related to files that she'd been working on before Nathan got her hooked on the Burchard case, but the majority were inquiries from prospective clients. She ought to be thankful that the work kept flowing her way. It was difficult not to feel overwhelmed at times, instead.

"I can handle some of those," Nathan offered.

Grateful, she passed him some of the new client

queries. Not too many, but enough to lighten her work-load for the next few weeks.

Nadine had watched the interplay with interest. Now she closed up her desk and grabbed her purse. "I should be going. It's after five and I have to be some-where."

She exchanged a quick, meaningful look with Nathan, and Lindsay was reminded of her earlier im-pression that these two had been discussing something important when she'd walked in.

"What's going on here?" She glanced from one to the other.

"Huh?" Nadine was suddenly all innocence as she slipped on her Burberry trench coat. "I don't know what you mean. I do have to run." Before disappearing out the door she added, "Have a good weekend. See you Mon-day."

After the door closed, there was a moment of silence. Lindsay reflected that she should ask Nadine to take her shopping one day. She'd never had the knack of find-ing sales, but Nadine was obviously great at it.

She turned to Nathan. "You two were having a pretty intense conversation when I walked in."

"Just personal stuff." He lifted one shoulder as if to say their conversation would be of little interest to her.

And perhaps it wouldn't. At any rate, they had more interesting stuff to talk about. "We should compare notes. Were you able to find out anything about Paige's past?"

"I was. Where should we go? Your office or mine?"

"Get real, Nathan. The working day is over." She opened the front door. "Time to hit the bar."

"Why don't you just stock all the ingredients for a paralyzer at the office?" Nathan wasn't thrilled about hanging out at the Stool Pigeon again. He was starting to get hungry and if this meeting took as long as he thought it was going to take, he might be forced to order something that wasn't liquid.

Lindsay shook her head vigorously. "No alcohol at work. That's a line I refuse to cross."

"Why? So that you can pretend you don't have a drinking problem?" His tone was light, but the question wasn't totally in jest. He wondered if Lindsay ever sat down and calculated how much liquor she had in a week. From what he'd seen, it was quite a lot.

Wendy set their drinks on the table. Lindsay touched her glass to his, then deliberately held his gaze as she took her first swallow.

"Define *problem*."

He wasn't going to be drawn into this. Maybe he shouldn't have said anything in the first place. "I'm not your babysitter. If you don't think you have a problem, then you probably don't."

He could tell that Lindsay had expected a fight. Him backing down had caught her off guard.

"That's right," she said finally. "I don't have a problem. I drink after working hours, to relax, and that's it. Anyone with my level of job stress would understand."

He had her level of job stress, and he didn't need a drink every night, but he decided not to point that out. Instead, he downed his mineral water and tried to ignore the growling from his empty stomach.

"So, you went shopping for commercial real estate today," he prodded. "How did that go?"

Lindsay's face lit up. She leaned forward, hands splayed on the table between them. "I phoned first thing in the morning and asked if I could book an appointment with someone who had been with the company a long time. I lucked out and got a woman who was very chatty. Helena Johnson told me Paige moved here from New Hampshire about nine months ago."

"That jives with what I found out today. Paige Stevens was born and educated in New Hampshire. Did Helena tell you anything else?"

"Tons. She really doesn't like the woman. And I pretended that I'd had an appointment with her a few weeks ago and hadn't been happy. You know what Helena said?"

Like he could possibly stop her from telling him. "What?"

"She said she wasn't surprised since I wasn't an older, wealthy male. Apparently those are the only clients Paige bothers working with. Nathan, I think Paige is working at that firm so she can nab herself a rich husband."

"That fits with what I learned about her past. She grew up in a small town named Lancaster in the White Mountains. Her folks were poor and she didn't go to school past high school. She married well, though, a widower with large landholdings and grown children. Apparently he was beset with digestive problems—which hadn't existed prior to the marriage—for quite a while before finally passing away one year ago."

"How did you find out all of this?"

"As I was telling Nadine, earlier, the Internet is a lovely thing. So are small town newspapers."

"Digestive problems, huh? Would I be crazy to consider the possibility that she may have been poisoning him?"

"I talked to a lot of people on the phone today, including the local sheriff. Nothing was considered suspicious at the time. But then I found someone who told me Paige had been having an affair with the sheriff."

"So much for his impartiality, then."

"Exactly what Paige's sister-in-law said. She was out of the country when her brother died, but she said she would have insisted on an inquest if she'd been here. Her brother had never been sick a day, before he married Paige."

"Circumstantial."

"Very," Nathan agreed.

"But still, very interesting." She raised her hand and made eye contact with Wendy on the other side of the room. When Wendy arrived with a fresh paralyzer, he asked if they served any salads.

The older woman tucked aside a strand of hair that had escaped her ponytail. "Sure, we have house salad and Caesar."

"Could I get the house salad with the dressing on the side?"

Wendy exchanged a "well, isn't he a fussy one" look with Lindsay, then went back to the kitchen.

Lindsay seemed amused by his order. "Jeez, Nathan, couldn't you just once eat a burger and fries. Or at least a clubhouse sandwich? You know, Man Food."

Nathan leaned back a little in his chair. "I don't need to eat a hunk of grilled meat to prove my masculinity."

Amusement sparked an extra glow in her eyes. "Is that so?" she asked softly.

He indulged in a long, intimate look at her. The words *beautiful* or *pretty* couldn't come close to describing her. She had a quality that was…iridescent. Her translucent skin glowed. Her pale eyes shimmered. The contrast between her delicate exterior, and the energy and fire within, was irresistible.

Nathan was a man of reason and logic.

Usually.

"Would you like me to prove that I'm a man? 'Cause I can definitely do that."

CHAPTER TEN

"NATHAN, STOP IT." LINDSAY took a drink, then coughed as the liquid went down the wrong way. "This is a working meeting, for God's sake."

"You're the one who questioned my virility," he pointed out. "I had to defend myself as a point of honor."

His salad arrived and Lindsay didn't say another word about so-called "Man Food" as he set about eating it, though he could tell she was biting back a comment as she watched him add only half the dressing to the greens.

"The love nest?" he prodded. "You said you checked it out this afternoon?"

"Right. I met with the building manager after lunch." She snapped back into work mode, leaning in toward him, her hands moving expressively with each word. "I said I was in the market for an apartment, preferably on the top floor."

"Clever."

She nodded. "He informed me that the entire upper floor is being leased by the owner of the building."

"Surprise, surprise."

"I asked when the lease would expire and he said six more months." She frowned. "I expected it would be longer."

"It's not like Maurice will have a problem renewing if the affair lasts that long."

"Or maybe he has no intention of renewing either way. Maybe he asked Audrey for a divorce because he plans to marry Paige."

"He certainly looked pretty head over heels about her last night. But I wouldn't be so sure about marriage."

"Paige is smart. She'll be looking for some way to lock him in. Maybe get pregnant?" she mused.

"That would be some trick. Paige Stevens had her tubes tied before she married Mr. New Hampshire."

Lindsay gaped. "How on earth did you find out that?"

"Hey, that's my specialty. Uncovering other people's secrets."

"Impressive work, Fisher."

He wondered what she'd say if she knew he'd uncovered one of *her* secrets today, too. The fact that she'd changed her last name was still difficult for him to fathom. Perhaps Nadine was right and Lindsay had found Yzereef too awkward to spell and pronounce. The Lindsay he knew wouldn't change her identity for such a superficial reason.

If people had trouble pronouncing and writing her name, she'd say that was *their* problem.

No, there had to be some other reason. Possibly connected to her parents' deaths, but not necessarily.

He pushed aside his empty salad plate. He'd had enough talk about work. He wanted to continue where they'd left off the other night. Getting to know each other.

"I got an invitation in the mail yesterday from my

alma matter. NYU is holding a series of lectures on the history of criminology for alumni. You ever go to stuff like that?"

She shook her head.

"Where did you go to school, by the way? I don't recall you talking about it."

He'd thought he'd done a good job of slipping the question in, all natural and casual, like.

But Lindsay wasn't fooled. She glared at him. "In California." Then she put some money on the table. More than enough to cover her two drinks. "I should get going."

"Don't you want some dinner? How about I treat you to one of those potpies you love so much."

"I thought maybe I'd order pizza tonight for a change."

He didn't think that had been her plan fifteen minutes ago. He put down some money, too, then slid out of the booth seat after her. "I'll walk you home."

"Give it a rest, Fisher. I'm just down the block." She pulled her jacket close to her body and brushed past him.

He noticed Wendy, and her husband Mark, watching with concern.

"You okay, Lindsay?" Mark called out.

She waved dismissively. "You bet. I'll see you tomorrow night."

Out on the street, Lindsay sunk her hands into her jacket pockets and hunched her shoulders against the cold wind. Nathan had to hurry to keep up with her.

"What's the story with Mark and Wendy?" he asked, just to make small talk.

"No story, as far as I know. When I moved in three years ago, they were already operating the Stool Pigeon. As far as I know, they've owned it a long time."

"So…did they meet in Manhattan? Do they have children?"

"No idea." She fumbled with her door key and he took it from her.

"What are you doing? Give that back."

"I will in a minute. Tell me something first."

"Stop playing games. I'm tired."

At seven-thirty in the evening? He didn't think so. She'd been full of energy and enthusiasm when they'd been discussing the case. "Did it bother you that I asked where you went to college?"

"Of course not." She tried to laugh, but he wasn't fooled. He sensed something lonely and sad in her and it puzzled him how one simple question seemed to have affected her so strongly.

"How come you don't like talking about your past?"

"Jeez, Fisher. Why the inquisition? Who cares what school I went to—what could it possibly matter?"

She pulled back slightly, and their gazes met. Her eyes were luminous, wide and full of emotion. He thought he could see desire mixed in with the anger, but maybe he was just kidding himself.

"This isn't about any one specific fact," he said. "Sometimes I wonder what I'd learn if I did a background check on *you*."

She went very still. Then she grabbed the key out of his hand. "If you ever did that, Nathan, then everything between us would be over. Our partnership. Our friendship. Everything."

A moment later, she had disappeared inside her building.

SHE NEEDED A DRINK.

Lindsay opened her fridge. Every ingredient to mix a paralyzer was in here: tequila, vodka, coffee liqueur, cola and cream. But tonight, she wasn't in the mood for measuring and mixing. She grabbed the bottle of tequila. As she untwisted the cap, she considered drinking straight from the bottle, but that seemed a little too desperate, so she grabbed a juice glass from the cupboard and poured two fingers' worth of the amber brew.

Nathan. Damn the man, he had her so confused. As long as they were working, everything was fine. But then he'd cross a line—make her aware of him as a man, not just a partner—and all bets were off.

She was inconveniently, incredibly, undeniably attracted to him.

Clearly working together was going to be impossible. Somehow she had to get through the month, though. Once they'd done as much as possible to help Audrey Burchard, then she would tell him. Nathan would find work somewhere else, she would regain control of her life and everything in general would return to normal.

God, how depressing.

Lindsay took a long swallow of the tequila.

Don't think about him. Not now.

She wished she could just keep drinking the tequila until she fell into a stupor, but long ago she'd made a promise to her sister and it was something she took seriously. She allowed herself to finish the glass, then poured another and put the bottle away.

She called for a pizza and watched TV until the delivery guy arrived. When she finally had food in her system, she decided she might as well get some work done. She already knew this wasn't going to be a good night for sleep.

As she sat by the computer in her living room, she tried not to remember that just one night ago Nathan had been sitting in this very chair…

Stop it, Lindsay. Focus on helping somebody else.

Those messages Nadine had given her earlier. She had them in her bag somewhere. Lindsay fished through all her papers until she found them. She selected one at random.

Nadine had filled out a preliminary case summary, along with a woman's name and phone number. Apparently this woman had met a man while holidaying in Florida. They'd fallen in love and he'd asked her to marry him, but the woman wisely wanted to check out the guy first.

On paper the guy sounded great. Albert Walker-Smythe had a degree from the University of Florida and worked as an accountant in a large, reputable firm. So far so good.

But then Lindsay read the P.S. Nadine had added to the end of the message…*the wedding is in one week.*

Lindsay groaned. Normally she would call the woman back, arrange a meeting, request a retainer and make sure the check cleared the bank before even starting a case like this.

But there was no time and the consequences were too high. She'd do a few quick searches now. If the guy seemed legit, she'd call the woman tomorrow and follow standard procedure.

It took Lindsay only fifteen minutes to realize that Walker-Smythe was a total scam artist. Not only had he lied about his university education, but he'd omitted mentioning his criminal record. Shaking her head, Lindsay jotted some notes for the phone call she would be making tomorrow morning. Topping the list was her first recommendation: Cancel the wedding!

By the time she'd finished her notes, her eyes were burning and the back of her skull had started to throb. She checked the time. It was almost one in the morning.

She tried stretching out on the sofa, but that only made her think of Nathan again. Damn, she wanted another drink.

Instead, she ran a bath, lit some candles and put Shelby Lynne on the sound system. The idea was to relax, but after Lindsay had soaped herself clean, she was too uptight to sit and soak.

Giving up on the bath routine, she drained the tub and wrapped her pink, warm body in a terry cloth robe.

She'd try sleeping again. In the bed this time.

But the old sadness was rolling in and she found herself doing something she never would have expected. She reached for her phone and dialed Nathan's home number.

CHAPTER ELEVEN

WHAT ARE YOU DOING? THIS IS crazy. Hang up, fast, before he—

"Hello? Lindsay? Is that you?"

Immediately she felt like an idiot. Why should he care that she couldn't sleep? It wasn't his problem.

"Lindsay? Are you okay?"

"Do you remember the night we were working late tailing the punk with the mermaid tattoos?"

He picked up the story without hesitation. "We were in an unmarked Buick. It was raining."

She closed her eyes. "It was so bloody hot and muggy in that car. And you couldn't find anything good on the radio."

"And then, suddenly, that James Blunt song came on."

"'Beautiful.'" The song had been playing everywhere that year, but that night she'd felt as though she was hearing it for the very first time.

Then Nathan had looked at her.

And she'd been lost.

Though she'd denied it, what had happened between them had been a big part of the reason she'd left the force three weeks later.

"Lindsay." His voice sounded thick with emotion. "Should I come over?"

She ignored the part of her mind that handled logic and reason, listening instead to the aching need that she could no longer deny.

"Yes."

"I'm leaving now."

She waited by the window, somehow not surprised to see that it had started raining since the pizza had been delivered. She opened the window a crack so she could smell the freshness and hear the soothing drumming as the city underwent a thorough cleansing.

After only fifteen minutes or so, she saw a tall figure in a dark coat walking up the street. The man stopped at her building and looked up to her third-floor window. Nathan. She wrapped an arm around her waist and shivered, though she wasn't cold.

She was nervous. She didn't entertain men in her apartment very often. Emotional attachments were too problematic, and the idea of inviting a man she didn't know very well into her home just seemed plain unsafe to her. So it had been a long time since she'd....been with somebody.

Not that she'd invited Nathan here to have sex.

No?

Well, maybe it had sort of been implied. But she could still change her mind. Nathan would respect that.

She pressed the security code to let him in, then opened the apartment door. As soon as she saw him, she started to apologize. "I'm sorry I called so late."

"I couldn't sleep, either."

His hair and face were soaked and water droplets

shimmered on his black jacket. He removed the coat in the hall, shook off most of the water, then stepped inside.

"Let me take that."

"It's wet. Let me. Then we can talk."

She'd felt a physical rush of pleasure when he'd removed his jacket. A gray T-shirt stretched over his muscular chest and faded blue jeans hung low on his hips. His face might be of the wholesome variety, but his body was pure masculine power...strong, tight and hard, in perfect shape.

She put a hand to the collar of her robe, suddenly wondering why she hadn't thought to get dressed. Being in her robe like this was a little obvious, wasn't it?

Embarrassed, she tried to distract herself. "Would you like a drink?"

"No."

His eyes sought out hers, and she shivered again under his tender scrutiny. For a tough guy, Nathan had a real gentle side—something she'd always admired about him.

She waited for him to touch her, trembling again as she imagined his arms slipping under her robe, around her back.

But he didn't make a move toward her. He didn't say anything, either, just stood patiently, watching her. Under his warm, intent gaze, she suddenly felt shy.

Shy—her? What a laugh. She tilted her head toward the kitchen. "Maybe you don't want one, but I could definitely use a drink."

"Allow me." He went to the kitchen and pulled out the various bottles and cartons that were lined up on the top shelf of her fridge.

"Sorry I don't have any mineral water," she ribbed him, but he didn't smile.

"It isn't a mineral water sort of night."

Her chest muscles tightened at his words, his serious tone. She was tempted to ask him what sort of night it was, then. But she didn't dare. Every skin cell on her body was vibrating with the sensual need to be stroked. And while normally she had no problem making the first move in a sexual encounter, tonight her instincts were warning her to hold back.

She watched Nathan pour measured amounts of liquids into two glasses, creating the perfect, creamy balance. Other than the wine they'd shared at dinner last night, Nathan had never drank alcohol in her presence. At least he hadn't in the past.

Tonight was apparently to be an exception.

They settled with their drinks in the living room. Nathan waited for her to sit first, then chose a spot close, but not touching her.

The empty space between them, though small, surprised her.

Maybe he wasn't here for sex. She looked at him, puzzled, trying to see the answer in his eyes. But he wasn't giving away anything by his expression. He set his drink on the table, then rested his hands on his thighs.

Lindsay put down her drink, too.

"I need you to talk to me, Lindsay."

"About what?" she asked, her nervousness mounting.

"Anything, as long as it isn't related to work."

"What else is there?"

"Your hobbies? Your interests?"

"I run a couple times a week and go to the occasional yoga class. When I was younger I was really into judo. And you?"

"I run, too. And I belong to a gym at the end of my block. I share hockey tickets with some buddies I went to school with. And I like to have dinner on Sundays with my sister and nephew."

She thought of something else she could contribute. "Every Saturday I have lunch with my sister. So. Is that enough sharing?"

"I want to know you, Lindsay. The *real* you. The *complete* you."

His words shattered something hard and tight inside of her. To her surprise, a tear leaked out from one eye. She brushed away the moisture.

No one had ever said anything like that to her before.

And the look in his eyes. Pure compassion and caring. No hint of the morbid curiosity that she despised so much.

But why should he be curious? He didn't know what had happened. Thank God, he didn't know. She closed her eyes, searching for strength, for balance and perspective.

Her sister thought she'd erected a wall between herself and the rest of the world. Meg kept telling Lindsay that eventually the wall would have to come down.

Lindsay didn't agree. She was stronger than her sister and so she was able to face the brutal truth. What had happened to her and Meg had left a scar that could never go away. What Nathan seemed to be offering...complete understanding and empathy...was impossible.

But there was something else he could give her,

something she'd never wanted from a man before. Not just sex, but intimacy and caring.

"You *do* know me. We worked together for over a year."

He sighed. "You're not understanding on purpose. But I'm willing to take baby steps. Start with one piece of information about your past. Can you trust me that much?"

She fought the urge to argue that the past wasn't relevant. She knew that was a lie, and she didn't want to insult him. "One fact? I grew up in rural California and went to university at Berkley. Satisfied?"

"Like I said, it's a start. Now it's my turn. I grew up in Manhattan with my parents and my sister. My dad was a firefighter. I've already told you he died saving someone from a burning building. I was twelve when that happened. I'm guessing you were even younger when your parents died."

She shrugged.

"But you don't want to talk about that, right?"

"Right," she agreed.

"So what is it you want, Lindsay? Just sex?"

In the past, yes. With Nathan it was already too late to keep their relationship so contained. "Work partners with benefits," she decided was the best way to put it.

"No strings, no promises."

She nodded.

Their gazes met and without looking away Nathan slid closer. His hand slipped along her cheek, to cup the back of her head. She loved the feeling of his fingers combing through her hair, the combination of strength and gentleness in his hand.

He studied her face with loving intensity. She waited, breathless, feeling a shocking vulnerability and an aching need.

He finished his perusal of her face with her eyes, gazing deeply into them, and then, slowly, he angled his mouth toward hers.

She gasped with the initial pleasure of lips meeting lips. And then she angled her face, too, allowing for a closer connection.

The chemistry was instantaneous, just as it had been the first time. Sensation blocked out rational thought and she allowed herself to react on the physical level, kissing him, reaching her arms around his back as he did the same with her.

Eventually passionate kisses tapered to something softer and exploratory. He pressed his mouth to her eyes, to her cheekbones, to the bridge of her nose.

Time ticked away unnoticed as she explored the masculine beauty of his face, too, with her lips, the tips of her fingers. She couldn't believe she was doing this. Kissing Nathan. Her partner. Ex-partner. Now partner, again.

And then she felt him tugging at her robe. The soft cotton parted and his hands slid along her rib cage to explore the length of her back.

"Stand up."

She did as he asked, and he moved with her. His hands slipped lower down her body, cupping her butt, then pressing her to him.

She loved feeling how aroused he was. She dipped her fingers inside his waistband until she found the fastening for his jeans, the fullness at his zipper.

"Here? Or the bedroom?" he asked.

The idea of moving apart, even for just a few seconds, was agony. "Here."

He slipped the robe over her shoulders and it fell to the floor. Moments later his jeans, his T-shirt, joined it.

Nathan stood back, his gorgeous body glowing in the faint city light that spilled in between the slats of her wooden blinds. She couldn't wait to touch him, to taste him, to see what logical, rational Nathan would do when his body was pulsing with pleasure.

"You are so beautiful, woman."

"Thanks for noticing."

He laughed at her confidence and she raised her eyebrows. She'd always been happy with her body. Why pretend otherwise?

Last night Nathan had used a blanket from her bed to cover her while she slept on the sofa. Now he spread that same blanket on the floor and they tumbled onto it, his skin warm and smooth next to hers. He settled her onto her back, then propped himself above her. With tender hands, he cupped one breast, then the other, kissing her hardened nipples, testing them with his teeth.

She moaned to show him what she liked. It seemed as if she liked *everything*. She relaxed and enjoyed for a while, then put a hand to his chest.

"My turn," she said.

He took her hand and placed it over her head, pinning it there with one long, muscled arm. "No rush, sweetheart," he said softly. "We've got all night."

Finally. An advantage to having insomnia.

LINDSAY'S INCREDIBLE ENERGY and enthusiasm made her a wonderful partner in bed. The sex was incendiary between them, but Nathan hoped she had also sensed his caring and his tenderness. She'd only trusted him with a nugget from her past, which made him all the more certain that something very painful still waited to be revealed.

He would be patient. He had no choice, since he now had no doubt that he dangled precariously on the verge of falling in love.

As the sky lightened with dawn, the rain stopped and they finally fell asleep. Lindsay rested with her head on his chest and one leg over his thighs. He was pinned like a butterfly, but he didn't mind. He drifted in and out of sleep for a few hours, grateful that Lindsay, at least, seemed to be getting uninterrupted rest for a change.

It was close to noon when she finally opened her eyes. Her dark lashes swept upward, then he heard a quick intake of breath.

"What time is it?"

He'd removed his watch, but there was a clock display on her DVD player. "Eleven-forty."

"Are you serious?"

She jolted upright, apparently not at all self-conscious that she was nude. He enjoyed the daytime view of her small, shapely breasts and the tight abdominal muscles of a woman who worked out regularly.

She untangled her legs from his, then brushed aside the blanket. "Why aren't you moving? We're late for work."

"It's Saturday."

"Oh. Right. That explains why the alarm didn't go off." She raked a hand over the top of her head, spiking up her thick blond hair.

"Come back to bed. Or should I say, the floor?" He reached for her, touching the side of her calf.

"I can't. My sister will be here in twenty minutes. I'm going to be late as it is." She dug around the clothes piled on the floor until she found her robe, which she slipped over her shoulders. She shook her head as if she still felt a little foggy brained. "I didn't finish my drink."

She was looking at the paralyzer he'd mixed for her, still sitting on the coffee table. "You didn't touch your drink," he clarified.

"That's a first." She grabbed her glass and his, and carried them to the kitchen. He heard her dump the contents down the drain, then turn on the tap to rinse the glasses. She was back in the living room a moment later. "You need to leave."

He had to laugh at her bluntness. "No morning sex?"

"It's almost afternoon," she reminded him. "And my sister will be here in twenty minutes."

"I'd love to meet her."

She looked at him warily. "You're not coming to lunch with us."

"My treat."

"No way."

"It'll be fun." He pulled on his jeans. "Next week you can meet my sister."

"Stop it. We are not dating, we are not going to meet each other's family."

Her words might have been wounding, if he wasn't damn sure that last night had been as incredible for her as it had been for him.

"We have a deal," she reminded him. "Working partners with benefits."

"What about friendship?"

"Stop negotiating. It isn't fair."

And how she made him feel. Was that fair?

He stood and as he stretched out the kinks in his shoulders, he noticed Lindsay eyeing his body. Good. Let her remember just how good the sex had been.

"Do you want a quick shower before you leave?"

"Why don't you go first and I'll put on some coffee."

She planted her hands on her hips, exasperated. "You're not staying long enough for coffee."

"We drink coffee together at work. Why not the morning after sex?" He moved close to her, ran his hands down either side of her body, then planted a wet kiss on the base of her neck. With satisfaction he registered her quiet moan. "We are going to do this again, right?"

"Maybe."

He ran his hands up this time, gently brushing her nipples, and kissed her again.

"Probably."

"Good. I'll make coffee." He went to the kitchen and looked through cupboards until he found a French coffee press.

Lindsay stood in the doorway, watching. "The beans are in the freezer," she finally said grudgingly. "I'm going to shower and when I get out you better be gone."

GREAT SEX, A SOLID STRETCH of sleep and no nightmares should have put her in a cheerful mood. But Lindsay felt stressed as she showered quickly, then chose a simple cashmere sweater and her favorite jeans to wear for her lunch with Meg.

She really needed Nathan to be gone before Meg showed up, because if her sister met him there would be messy complications. Meg was sure to like him, not the least because she'd been bugging Lindsay about finding a man ever since Lindsay's thirtieth birthday last April.

According to Meg, being single was fine for your twenties. But once you reached your thirties it was time to settle down. Meg could have theories like that because she was only twenty-seven.

Lindsay applied a minimal amount of make-up, strapped on her watch, then left her bedroom.

Please be gone, Nathan. Please...

But there he was, sitting at her kitchen table, sipping from her largest coffee mug. He was wearing the jeans and T-shirt from last night and frankly he looked every bit as sexy as he had then.

She turned her back on him and helped herself to the coffee.

"Look, Nathan—"

"I'll leave as soon as you give me one good reason why we shouldn't try a real relationship. We have interests in common, great chemistry and we're about the same age. If we input our data into a computer, I bet we'd be a very close match."

"But I'm not looking for a match."

"Why not? There isn't another man. I'd know if there were."

"You're right. There isn't a man in my life right now. And I'm good with that. It's how I want it."

"Really."

He didn't sound as if he believed her at all.

"A woman does not have to be involved with a man to have a happy, worthwhile existence."

"I'm sure that's true. But it's also possible to have a happy and worthwhile existence *with* one. So why rule out the possibility?"

She eyed the time displayed on the stove. Not good. Meg was already late. "Can we please have this conversation another time?"

Finally Nathan seemed to accept that she was serious. "Okay. Maybe this is too soon to meet your sister."

He left his coffee on the table and snagged his coat from the hook by the door. Lindsay was annoyed to discover that now that he had finally capitulated, she actually wanted him to stay.

Lindsay helped herself to the coffee, trying to pretend she was cool with the situation. An offhand goodbye and that was it.

But as Nathan opened the door to leave, he drew up short. Someone was already there, right at the threshold.

"Hi, there. I'm Meg. Are you a friend of my sister's?"

CHAPTER TWELVE

NATHAN INTRODUCED HIMSELF to Lindsay's sister. In person Meg seemed even more delicate and pretty than she had in the photographs. She made no attempt to hide her delight at having discovered a man in her sister's apartment.

"Nathan Fisher," she repeated his name thoughtfully. "Did you work with Lindsay when she was with the NYPD?"

"We were partners."

"That's right. I remember her talking about you."

That had him curious. "Good stuff, I suppose?"

Meg's gaze drifted to one side. "Oh…mostly." Her roving eyes picked up on the blanket pooled on the living room floor. She smiled knowingly. "Looks like you two have reconnected."

Lindsay whisked by them both, grabbed the blanket and tossed it on the sofa. "Nathan and I are working on a case together. It's a temporary thing."

A shadow flickered over Meg's face, then was replaced with determined cheerfulness. "Temporary or not, Nathan, you're welcome to join us for lunch. Unless you have plans?"

"No plans," he said, deliberately not checking in

Lindsay's direction. "I'd love to join you, but I think Lindsay was looking forward to a private lunch."

"Nathan was just on his way out," Lindsay concurred.

"But I never get to meet your friends," Meg protested.

"Like I already explained, we just work together."

"Right. Funny, but I never have overnighters on a blanket in my living room with the people I work with." Meg grabbed her sister's hand with one hand, Nathan's arm with the other. "Come on, Lindsay. I may be your younger sister, but I haven't been that naive in years."

Nathan let himself be pulled out to the hall by Meg. He liked Lindsay's sister's style. He had a feeling there were a lot of things about her that he was going to like.

ONLY ONCE THEY WERE OUT on the street did Meg let go of Nathan's hand.

"So where are we headed?" he asked.

"We have a standing reservation at Jo Jo's." From her tone it was clear that Lindsay still felt resentful about his presence.

"I know the place." It was about eight blocks away, close to the Museum of Natural History and facing Central Park. "Should I hail a cab?" The women were wearing very high heels with their jeans, and he didn't imagine they would be comfortable walking, but both of them turned down his offer.

Lindsay set the pace and it was faster than Nathan would have expected. As they walked, Meg kept the conversation moving, too.

"Did you grow up in New York?" she asked.

"Yeah. My dad worked for the fire department and my mom taught piano."

"Do you have any brothers or sisters?"

"A sister, Mary-Beth. She and her son, Justin, are living with me right now, though they'll be moving out soon. I have a two-bedroom apartment in Morningside Heights, which is handy for her. She teaches at Columbia."

"Lindsay and I lived together when we first moved to New York—until she kicked me out of the nest." Meg reached over to poke her sister in the arm.

Lindsay ignored the jab. In fact, she seemed to be doing her best to ignore the entire conversation.

"She said we were getting too dependent on one another," Meg continued. "Which was probably true. She's always been the stronger one."

"Where did you get your law degree?" he asked. It was such a delight to finally be talking to someone who didn't hoard her words.

"Lindsay and I both took our undergrad degrees at Berkley. Then she moved with me to Boston so I could study law at Harvard. I owe her a lot for that one."

"You paid most of your way with scholarships," Lindsay interjected, proving that she was listening, after all.

"We had some insurance money for our education, too. Did Lindsay explain…?"

"Meg, you chatterbox. Give Nathan a chance to get a word in edgewise, would you?"

Nathan realized this was Lindsay's way of telling her sister that she *hadn't* explained. Too bad he was falling for the wrong sister. It seemed that Lindsay held everything in, while Meg did the exact opposite.

Glancing at her sister, Meg apologized. "I do talk too much. It's a failing of the legal profession. So tell me more about your parents. Are they still living?"

"I'm afraid not. My father died on the job when I was twelve and Mom passed away about five years ago."

"That must have been hard," Meg sympathized.

"We were a close family and, yeah, it was hard." Nathan wondered if this was why Lindsay hadn't wanted him along for lunch—she'd been worried Meg would talk too much. But most of this—information about families and where you grew up and went to school—was usual fodder for conversation between new acquaintances.

When they arrived at the restaurant, a third chair was added to a table on the patio overlooking the park, without fuss. Nathan waited for both ladies to be seated, then made himself comfortable opposite them.

Lindsay shifted her water glass from one spot to another, leaving a wet ring on the linen tablecloth behind. He could tell she was tense. Probably wondering what family "secrets" her sister would reveal next.

But now that they were in the restaurant, Meg had become quiet. She studied the menu anxiously and questioned the waiter carefully about several items before making her choices.

Nathan wondered if she obsessed about her weight. If so, he couldn't understand why. She was even thinner than her sister and he could personally attest to the fact that Lindsay carried no extra pounds on her sexy, athletic body.

Once their food was served, however, Meg relaxed again. She started talking about her work, and soon Lindsay was drawn into the conversation, as well.

After Meg had explained a complicated legal case involving an estate settlement, Lindsay leaned across the table and told him, "My sister is a tiger in the courtroom."

"Oh, hardly." Still, Meg seemed pleased by the compliment, as she carefully sliced a tiny piece of fat from the salmon fillet she'd ordered.

Though she was subtle about it, Nathan noticed Lindsay watched every bite that Meg ate. When the waiter came to ask if they wanted dessert Nathan expected both women to decline. But after a glance at her sister, Meg ordered a fruit plate.

"I'm having the torte." Lindsay handed the dessert menu to the server decisively.

When the desserts arrived, Lindsay dove into her cake with gusto, while Meg picked carefully at the fruit. Eventually, both plates were empty and Lindsay leaned back with satisfaction.

Nathan excused himself from the table and went in pursuit of the bill. Once he'd settled their tab, he returned to the table and found Meg sitting alone.

As soon as he sat down, she leaned toward him.

"You like my sister, don't you?"

"It's that obvious?"

Meg smiled. "She likes you, too."

"She has a funny way of showing it."

"I know." Meg sighed, exasperated. "My sister is the most stubborn, independent person I've ever known. She's always been that way, even before...well, she just always has."

Noticing Lindsay on her way back to the table, Meg stopped talking and reached for her purse.

"So what now?" Nathan asked, wondering if the sisters planned to spend the entire day together.

"I have to go home and walk my dog," Meg said.

"What about you, Lindsay? Want to catch a movie?"

"No time," she replied briskly. "I have a lot of errands."

"Later in the afternoon, she goes for a run," Meg interjected helpfully.

"Shut up, Meg."

The three of them walked Meg to the entrance of the subway. Once her sister was gone, Lindsay seemed to expect that he would leave, as well.

"See you at the office on Monday."

"Is that really what you want?" He took her hands and pulled her close so he could see her expression when she answered him.

She could brush him off now, if she wanted. But *she* had been the one to call *him* last night.

"No... But... Look, Fisher, I need to keep this simple." The autumn breeze ruffled Lindsay's blond hair provocatively, reminding him of how she had looked last night when they were making love. Her skin, already slightly pink from the walk and the sunshine, turned a shade darker under his scrutiny.

Why this woman? he found himself wondering. She made nothing easy. He ought to be running in the opposite direction. And yet he was more fascinated than ever.

"It doesn't have to be complicated," he said. "Why don't you take care of those errands, then meet me for a run around four o'clock. We can grab some dinner later. How does that sound?"

"Fun," she admitted. "Maybe that's what scares me."

AFTER SHE'D PICKED UP HER dry cleaning and a few groceries, Lindsay went home to go through her mail and pay bills. Around four o'clock she changed into shorts and a Dri-Fit T-shirt. When she was ready, she stuck a key into her pocket, then jogged out of her building and along West Seventy-ninth toward the park.

She felt strong, alive…happy. She knew her good mood had a lot to do with the fact that she had plans with Nathan. Meg was right—she needed more in her life than just her sister and her work.

Maybe this new deal she had worked out with Nathan would be perfect. Sex without emotional obligations. Partners—with benefits.

Rounding the corner, Lindsay spotted Nathan waiting at the edge of the park. He hadn't seen her yet—he was diverted by the antics of a squirrel in the branches above his head. Seeing him laugh at something so innocent, gave her an aching feeling in her chest. There was an essential goodness to Nathan that spoke to her. And made her doubly angry about the way the NYPD had shafted him.

"Hey, there!" She waved as she crossed the street, and catching sight of her Nathan smiled and waved back. He pushed off from the tree he'd been leaning against and jogged toward her, moving with the seemingly effortless stride of a natural runner.

They caught up on the path heading north and Lindsay pushed her pace a little, not willing to have him slow down on her account.

"Did you see that squirrel?" Nathan asked. "I swear, he was dropping acorns on my head on purpose."

Lindsay laughed. He was such a softie. "Don't lie. I saw you feeding him."

"I happened to have a few peanuts in my pocket." Nathan veered to the left as the path divided in front of them. "Five miles okay?"

"You bet."

An hour later they were back at her apartment, flushed and sweaty. Lindsay tossed her keys on the counter and they landed with a clatter. "Dibs on the shower," she said, kicking off her running shoes. Before she'd taken two steps, Nathan's arms were around her.

Normally she wasn't into kissing sweaty men, but Nathan proved the exception. When he pressed his mouth to hers, she parted her lips willingly. He slid his hands under her T-shirt, lifting it over her head in one slick motion. A moment later she'd disposed of his shirt, too, so she could press herself right against his hot torso.

They had sex right there in the hall—sweaty, hot, after-running sex. Then they moved to the shower for steamy, hot, soapy-clean sex. When they were done, she sank to the floor of the shower, utterly spent.

The next thing she knew, Nathan was shampooing her hair. He stood behind her so she could rest her back against his legs while his fingers massaged her scalp deeply in slow circular movements. The combination of Nathan's touch and hot water was heavenly.

"Hey, there. You're falling asleep." Nathan's voice was warm and soothing. "I know a better place for that."

He eased her into a standing position, wrapped her in a big towel and led her to the bedroom. The two of them curled like puppies amid pillows, wrinkled sheets and her lightweight duvet. Lindsay snuggled into all of it, her mind in a delightful stupor, not induced by alcohol for a change but running, sex, heat and Nathan.

What an amazing combination.

They dozed for at least an hour and when Lindsay woke up, she was starving.

"Chinese food," Lindsay said, pushing aside Nathan's arm, which was draped over her waist. She grabbed her phone and hit Speed Dial. "What would you like?"

Nathan answered without opening his eyes. "Stir-fried chicken and veggies and steamed rice."

"Of course." She rolled her eyes, but gave the order exactly as he'd asked, then requested ginger beef and sweet and sour shrimp, as well.

"I hope you don't expect me to kiss you after that."

"No. I expect you to go home after that. It's been a long day, Fisher. I'm getting tired of you."

In one quick second he was out of bed, tackling her to the floor and kissing her for a long, delicious interlude.

When they were both completely out of breath, he helped her to her feet.

"Getting tired of me, huh. Say it again, Fox. And this time try to sound like you mean it."

LINDSAY WAS IN THE PLAYROOM again. She and Meg were molding clay animals for their make-believe zoo. Yesterday their father had cut out cardboard fencing which they had used to create pens for the lions and giraffes and bears. Their mother had spread a blue napkin in one corner. That was going to be the pond for the hippos and crocodiles.

As she pinched the clay with her fingers, trying to form a snout on her hippo, Lindsay's stomach started to ache. She knew something bad was about to happen. Something really, really bad.

And then she heard the screams. First her mom. Then her dad.

Meg froze with fear. *Stay here,* Lindsay told her sister. *Don't move.*

And now she was in the dark room, the room with all the blood. Her mother was on the floor. Her dad was holding a gun.

Lindsay? he said. *"Lindsay?"*

And then her sister screamed...

CHAPTER THIRTEEN

"LINDSAY." SOMEONE NEW WAS speaking her name. She didn't recognize his voice.

"Lindsay," he said again. "Wake up. You're having a nightmare."

Wait a minute. Yes, she knew the voice. It was Nathan Fisher. They'd fallen asleep after watching a movie. It was Saturday night—no, Sunday.

"Are you all right, sweetheart?"

She felt his hand brush over her forehead.

"You're drenched. And you were mumbling in your sleep."

What had she said? Please nothing that he would understand. She slid out of his arms to the edge of the bed, then stood and headed for the bathroom. At the sink she splashed water on her face. When she lifted her gaze, she could see Nathan's reflection in the mirror, behind her.

He passed her a towel. "Do you have nightmares often?"

She shrugged. "Often enough."

His arms circled her waist. "Come back to bed and tell me about it."

As if. "I'd rather clear my head first." She pried his

fingers from her body and headed toward the computer. "You go ahead and sleep."

Being Nathan, of course he didn't listen to her. She could sense him behind her, brooding, as she sat at her desk and booted up the computer.

"Don't tell me you're going to work."

"Might as well. I'm awake now."

The floorboards creaked as he headed to the kitchen. She heard him open the fridge, then a few moments later put something in the microwave. She did her best to tune him out.

Three new messages were in her in-box, all from that new client who was thinking of getting married. Lindsay had called her yesterday and had set up a meeting for Monday morning. But it seemed this woman was having second thoughts.

"I feel like an idiot for doubting the man I love. Let's just forget the whole thing. Of course, I'll pay for whatever time you've already spent…"

The second message, sent three hours after the first read, "Please confirm that you've received this e-mail. Also, could you please not phone my house…"

Finally, the last e-mail: "You know what? I think I will meet with you tomorrow after all. Just ignore my previous—"

Lindsay deleted all three messages without responding. Some clients. Tomorrow's meeting was not going to be pretty.

"Enough work." Nathan was back in the room, a mug in his hand. "I made you something. You can drink it in bed."

"You're awfully bossy."

"Come on, Lindsay. You're going to be beat tomorrow if you don't get some more rest."

She probably would have ignored him, but that last client had been so annoying she decided to cave. "Fine. But I'm only doing this because you mixed me a drink. What is it? A hot toddy?"

"Come and see." He waited until she was settled under the covers before he handed her the mug.

Lindsay took one taste, then made a face. "Hot cocoa." She started to get up. "It would be okay if we added some liqueur..."

"C'mon Lindsay. Just drink it. Save your recipe critique for the morning." He sank into bed beside her and turned out the light.

"Okay, fine. But I want you to know I'm just being polite. This stuff is awful."

"You are so polite, it's mind-boggling." Nathan closed his eyes and five minutes later he was fast asleep.

God, if only it could be that easy for her.

NATHAN DID HIS BEST TO KEEP exhaustion at bay as he pretended to sleep. He wanted to make sure Lindsay was asleep before he allowed himself that luxury. With nights like this, no wonder she was a little edgy at times.

He listened to her sip the last of the cocoa and place the mug on the bedside table. He half expected her to get out of bed again, but she sank under the covers. For a few minutes she tossed from one position to another. Finally she nudged up against him, and he looped his arm around her waist.

"Nathan?" she whispered.

"Yes."

"Talk to me."

She needed a distraction, he realized. He cast for a safe subject. "I remember the first time I went to a Yankees game. My dad took me on my seventh birthday…that was all I'd asked for. I didn't want a party, or present or cake. I just wanted to watch my heroes play ball."

She let out a long sigh, and as the air left her lungs he could feel her muscles relax.

"We had seats behind third base. I'll never forget how I felt in those electrifying seconds before the game began…"

He kept talking, reliving a happy memory that he hadn't thought about in a long time. He kept talking past the time he was certain she was asleep. Slowly he let his voice taper off. Then he looked down at her.

Her eyes were closed, her mouth was parted, her limbs were slack.

Definitely sleeping.

Finally.

Nathan let his eyelids relax and tried to do the same. He'd been deeply asleep when Lindsay woke up from her nightmare, but now, perversely, he was no longer tired.

Talking about his father had brought back a lot of memories. He wondered if his dad would think he'd done the right thing by leaving the force. Would he think that working for a private investigating firm was a worthwhile way to spend his life?

At the end of the day, son, you only have to answer to yourself…

Finally Nathan fell asleep.

LINDSAY AWOKE WITH A START when the alarm went off. She could feel Nathan behind her.

He'd spent the night. Again. She felt a buzz of panic and lifted his arm from her waist.

"Where are you going?" The muscles on his arm tightened. Suddenly his loose hold was a vise.

"Let go. We've got to get ready for work."

He kissed the back of her neck, then ran his hand over her hip and along the top of her thigh. His touch was silken and hot, but she refused to be seduced.

"I have a new client coming in at ten-thirty." She pushed against him and this time he didn't try to stop her. Once out of bed, she headed for the bathroom, grabbing her robe on the way.

In the shower, she finally faced what she had done.

She hadn't intended to spend her entire weekend with Nathan. Eating meals together, going on runs, watching movies…this was not the way their relationship was supposed to work. She was going to fall for the guy if she wasn't careful. It wouldn't be hard.

Nathan had a lot of good points, beyond his computer and bedroom skills. He was kind, had a great sense of humor and was fun to be around. Not to mention he mixed a mean paralyzer. Not that he'd utilized that skill much this weekend, she realized, thinking about the cocoa she'd had right before falling asleep.

God, cocoa. Was that what dating Nathan was bringing her to?

Dating Nathan.

Lindsay felt like pounding her head against the tiled bathroom wall.

Was she *insane?*

She'd gone from insisting she wanted to work alone, to agreeing to take Nathan on as a partner. Next she'd agreed that they could be partners "with benefits." Now dating?

The pendulum had definitely swung too far.

Lindsay emerged from the bathroom with her robe wrapped tightly around her. Nathan was just getting out from under the covers and she carefully avoided looking at his naked body as she surveyed the choices in her closet for something to wear. Nathan strode past on his way to the bathroom.

"The blue blazer brings out your eyes."

She'd been thinking of the blue, but chose the brown, instead. By the time she'd selected matching pants and a cream-colored, soft-as-silk T-shirt, Nathan was finished showering, shaving and dressing. She glanced at him, then away. Damn, did he have to look so good, this early in the day?

"You have clean clothes?"

"I keep the essentials in my briefcase."

"How convenient." She hated the jealous pang his words gave her. She shouldn't care about Nathan's past... or his future. She had no claim. She wanted no claim.

"A clean shirt and underwear come in handy after a night on surveillance when there isn't time to make it home before you're due at the office," Nathan added.

"No need to explain." And yet, she couldn't deny that she felt a rush of relief that Nathan didn't make a habit of these overnight encounters.

What had happened to her credo...no emotional attachments?

Lindsay grabbed her leather bag, checking to make

sure she had everything she needed for work. Finally, she grabbed her keys. "Ready to go?" she asked, not caring that she sounded like a drill sergeant, rather than a woman who'd spent two straight days in bed with this man.

"What about breakfast?"

"We'll have coffee at work."

"That's all you eat in the morning?"

She expelled her breath impatiently. "If you were expecting eggs, bacon and toast, you're in the wrong apartment."

"No kidding. I thought you said you bought groceries yesterday, but there's nothing in your kitchen."

"I bought the essentials," she insisted.

"Cream and cola," he shot back, "are not essentials."

"To me they are."

He sighed. "Your diet is seriously scary, you know that? But no worries. I'll pick up some bagels on the way to the office."

NADINE WAS AT THE COFFEE station when Lindsay pushed open the main door. Her receptionist was dressed in a stylish skirt and top, with patterned tights and a pair of short leather boots. The woman was always so well turned out. Lindsay tried to recall the last time *she'd* purchased a new outfit.

"Did you have a nice weekend?" Nadine asked.

Lindsay growled at the innocuous question and reached for the cup of coffee Nadine had just poured. She took a thankful sip and thought again about all the paralyzers she hadn't had that weekend.

No wonder she was in such a foul mood this morning.

On the other hand, her head actually felt clear, and her body light and springy. Of course, that might be due to the sex…

Nathan came in then, holding a brown paper bag of bagels up in the air like a trophy. "Breakfast for everyone. I've got cream cheese, too."

The sight of him had an unexpected effect on Lindsay's metabolism. She wanted to scream at herself. She'd seen him just five minutes ago…why did she have this happy, bouncy feeling just because he'd walked into the room?

"I hate cream cheese." She saw Nadine shoot her a surprised look. No wonder. Nadine knew she *loved* cream cheese.

Nadine helped herself to a bagel. "This was very thoughtful of you, Nathan."

Lindsay bit her tongue on the ungracious comment that popped into her head. She wanted to retreat to her office, but her stomach gurgled in protest. Though she rarely ate in the morning, today she happened to be ravenous. Perhaps because of her abstinence from alcohol, her overindulgence in sex, or a combination of the two. She chose a pumpernickel bagel and slathered it with cream cheese.

Neither Nadine nor Nathan made a comment about her professed dislike for the spread. They looked amused, though, and Nathan sidled up to her. "Eat lots, boss. Build up your stamina for later."

She shot him a warning look, but it was too late. Nadine tilted her head to one side and narrowed her oval-shaped green eyes. She studied Lindsay's face, then Nathan's.

"What's happening later?"

"Just work. I have a client, a Miss Carlene Schultz, coming in at ten-thirty. Show her to my office when she arrives, please."

Lindsay met Nathan's gaze one last time. *Watch yourself,* she warned him, silently. Then she took her breakfast into her office and closed the door.

As soon as Lindsay had left the room, Nadine turned to Nathan expectantly. "What's up with you two? And don't tell me nothing, because you have better chemistry than the interns on *Grey's Anatomy.*"

"You're hooked on that show, too?" he asked. "My sister got me started when she moved in a few months ago. What do you think the big cliff-hanger ending will be this season?"

"You don't want to talk about Lindsay, that's fine." She smiled. "But just so you know, I think it's great. You make an amazing couple."

"We aren't a couple."

"Did you have a fight already?"

"We're always fighting." He took a gulp of very black, very hot coffee and grimaced. "That isn't a good sign, is it?"

"With your average woman, no. But with Lindsay, it could be. She's got a very hard shell. At least you're getting under it."

Which might be a good thing. Or maybe not. He grabbed an extra bagel then started for his office. Partway there he paused. "You're going to tell her your real name soon, right?"

Nadine wrinkled her nose. "Do I have to?"

"It's almost the end of the month…you know what that means."

She straightened her shoulders, sucked in her breath. "Payday."

LINDSAY HAD FINISHED THE BAGEL, two cups of coffee and responded to five e-mails by the time Nadine admitted Carlene Schultz to her office.

Carlene looked around forty, attractive, with a long face and salon-coiffed hair. Judging by the quality of her business suit and her Patek Philippe watch, the woman had money.

Lindsay stood to shake her hand. Regardless of the size of the pocketbook, the standard spiel she gave her new clients was always the same and she ran through the ground rules with Carlene quickly. Carlene displayed a businesslike mind, combined with the emotions of a thirteen-year-old girl.

"I understand your terms and I accept them." She produced a Louis Vuitton wallet from her red leather purse and proceeded to write out a check for five hundred dollars.

"I feel so underhanded about this," Carlene confessed. "My Albert is such a sweetheart. He would be crushed if he thought I didn't trust him."

"Marriage entails serious legal obligations. If you own a house or investments…?"

Carlene nodded. "I do."

"Then you'd be foolish not to check out a few basic facts about someone you've only known a month."

"Albert doesn't care about my money. He isn't that sort of person."

Lindsay maintained a neutral expression with some difficulty. "Maybe not. But I strongly advise you to hold off on your wedding plans until I've had a chance to complete my preliminary check." She opened her appointment book. "I should have something for you by tomorrow."

"Wow, that's fast."

"In your message you mentioned getting married within a week."

Carlene nodded.

"Then we need to work fast." Lindsay stood to signal the meeting was over. "I'll call you tomorrow," she promised. "With a written report to follow soon after."

Lindsay walked Carlene through reception. As soon as her client had left, Nadine motioned for her attention.

"Celia Burchard arrived about ten minutes ago. She and Nathan are in the boardroom, waiting for you."

Lindsay was unhappy to feel an onrush of jealousy at the idea of Nathan alone with his former girlfriend. The emotion was totally juvenile, totally unprofessional. Was this what her weekend with Nathan had reduced her to?

"I TRIED TO CALL YOU AT HOME yesterday." Celia was pouting. There was no other way to describe it. "Your sister said you were out. That you'd been out all weekend."

Nathan wondered how much longer Lindsay would be busy with her client. "I'm sorry I missed your call. You should have tried my cell."

"I did."

"Oh. Right. I had it off most of the weekend." He rubbed the side of his face. This was damned awkward. He wasn't used to accounting for his whereabouts with former girlfriends. But this former girlfriend just happened to be a client.

"Where were you?"

"Um—"

Fortunately the door opened then and Lindsay breezed inside. "Sorry to keep you waiting." She shook Celia's hand then settled into the vacant chair at the head of the table. "I'm glad you decided to come in person for an update. We've had some interesting developments…"

"I'm not here to get an update," Celia interrupted. "I have news. Good news."

"Oh?" Lindsay glanced at him and he gave a small shrug, letting her know that he had no idea what Celia was about to tell them.

"My parents are getting back together. I'm here to terminate your services."

CHAPTER FOURTEEN

"I THOUGHT IT WOULD BE NICER to deliver the news in person," Celia continued, "rather than use the phone or send an e-mail."

Or maybe she'd just wanted to wound Nathan and see how he reacted, Lindsay guessed. If so, she must be disappointed at how unperturbed Nathan appeared by her pronouncement.

"Maybe you should listen to our update before you make that decision," he counseled her as if she were any other client.

"Your update is irrelevant now. I think the fact that I hired your agency to help Mom got my dad thinking. He must have realized how crazy he was acting. At any rate, he phoned Mom on Sunday and told her he's interested in a reconciliation."

Lindsay sat in stunned silence. This didn't make sense. The memory of Maurice Burchard fawning over Paige Stevens was still too vivid in her mind.

"They're going to spend the weekend at our Catskills lodge. Just the two of them. Isn't that romantic?"

Celia was clearly thrilled. "The best part," she added, "is that Dad is pretty sure that if he and Mom reconcile and he testifies in her favor, we can get the charges of attempted murder dropped entirely."

"Really." This abrupt reversal felt completely bogus to Lindsay. Glancing at Nathan, she could tell he had the same reservations.

"I don't want to dash your hopes," he said, "but I think you should consider the possibility that your father's interest in a reconciliation may not be sincere."

"Why would he lie?"

"I'm not sure. But there's something you need to see." Lindsay pulled her camera out of her bag. "I haven't had time to develop the pictures, but the view-finder should be big enough for you to recognize your father in these shots."

She handed Celia the camera so she could scroll through the photographs they'd taken at The Orange Tree restaurant.

Celia focused immediately on the redhead. "Who is that woman?"

"Her name is Paige Stevens. She's a real estate agent," Nathan explained. "We think she met your dad over a business deal five months ago."

Celia leaned closer to the camera, her expression turning to one of disgust. "That is definitely not a business meeting."

"No," Lindsay concurred.

Nathan pressed the arrow on the camera then held up a new picture for Celia to see. "After the meal we followed them to this apartment building."

"We checked into ownership of the building," Lindsay continued. "Your dad bought it last June. Paige Stevens was the real estate agent who brokered the deal. It's a rental property and your father and Paige jointly signed a six-month contract for the penthouse suite."

"No..." Celia shook her head. "I can't believe this." She pushed the camera away.

Lindsay expected Nathan to offer words of comfort. When he didn't, she stepped in. "I know this is a shock, Celia. I'm sorry we had to be the ones to tell you about your father's affair. But you hired us to find the truth. Unfortunately the truth is often uglier than we expect."

"I didn't know Dad was seeing another woman. I'm sure Mom didn't, either." Celia looked brokenhearted. Then she started to rationalize. "Dad must have ended his affair this weekend. Before he called Mom."

"I suppose it's possible." Nathan's tone was dubious. "But—"

"I can't believe he would talk to Mom about a reconciliation if he was still involved with another woman."

Talk about blind faith. Lindsay believed in making decisions based on objective facts. "Nathan and I could find out for sure."

Celia panicked. "That's not a good idea. I promised Dad I'd talk to you today and end our arrangement. If he realized you were still spying on him, he'd be furious."

Lindsay didn't like the sound of that. All her instincts screamed that something was wrong. "Are you sure you're comfortable with the idea of your parents going to the Catskills this weekend?" she asked.

"Of course. They need time alone to work things out."

"Last time they were alone, your mother shot your father," Lindsay pointed out.

"Not on purpose," Celia insisted. "Dad is finally willing to admit that it was just an accident. I don't know why you guys aren't happier about this. Don't you see…it's all working out."

Celia's eyes shimmered with emotion and Lindsay could empathize. Celia wanted desperately to believe that her family was about to be patched back together. That the embarrassing and distressing legal nightmare of her father's shooting was going to be packaged into a neat box labeled "accident."

"I hope you're right," Nathan said finally.

"I am." Celia ran a finger under her eyes, wiping away a tear along with the faint smudge of mascara. She smoothed her hair, then picked up her purse.

"I should go," she said. "It's almost time for me to drive Mom to her session."

Lindsay waited for Nathan to lead Celia out to reception. But he was lagging behind, fussing with some papers, so she took the lead.

"Feel free to call us if you sense something isn't right," she advised the younger woman as they shook hands at the door.

For the first time, Celia's eyes displayed a flicker of uncertainty. Then she raised her chin. "Everything's going to be fine."

"I hope so." Lindsay noticed Celia glance behind her. Nathan must have finally left the conference room. Celia seemed to be waiting for him to say something and when he didn't, her face pinkened.

Nathan moved up beside Lindsay. He touched her arm and said, "Come talk to me later, okay?"

"Sure."

The exchange between them was brief, nothing out of the ordinary. But Celia must have sensed undercurrents. Her eyes narrowed and she looked from Lindsay, to Nathan.

"She's your new girlfriend, isn't she? *She's* the reason you weren't home all weekend."

Lindsay instinctively pulled away from the other woman and glanced at Nathan, wondering what in the world he was going to say. Nathan looked miserable.

"Celia. This isn't the place—"

But Celia Burchard wasn't going to be shushed. Her eyes blazed with righteous indignation and she pointed her finger at his chest. "You should have told me your new partner was the reason you didn't want to get back together. I never expected you to be so sneaky and... cruel!"

She left, then, slamming the door behind her.

FOR A FEW SECONDS THE OFFICE felt uncomfortably quiet. Nadine was frozen at her desk, trying not to look or listen, her head bowed over the appointment book in front of her.

Poor kid. Nathan felt badly for her. She hadn't deserved to witness that crazy scene. None of them had.

He rubbed the side of his face, embarrassed, frustrated and more than a little angry. Celia had had no right to put on that scene. Their relationship had been over for months. And she'd been the one to end it.

He glanced over at Lindsay. She was standing in shooting stance, with her legs hip-distance apart, knees slightly bent and body squarely facing the target.

Him.

Clearly she had something on her mind.

"Um. I think I need to use the restroom. Excuse me."

Nadine slipped out of the office, carrying the key to the facilities down the hall.

As soon as she was gone, Lindsay started to speak, her voice tight and hard. "You and Celia were talking about getting back together? When?"

"A few days ago."

"And you never thought to mention anything? Hell, Nathan."

"It was before you and I—"

"You and I have nothing to do with this. Celia was our *client*. You told me your relationship with her was *over.*"

"And it was, damn it. When she asked me to meet her for coffee, I assumed she wanted to discuss her parents. How was I supposed to know she wanted to talk about…personal things? Frankly, it never occurred to me to tell you about it since I had no intention of getting back with Celia."

"This situation is totally out of hand. I knew when I woke up that we'd made a mistake. Until now, I didn't realize how bad it really was."

"You're blowing this out of proportion."

"Oh, really? I've worked hard to make this business a success. Fox Investigations may not mean anything to you, but it's my *life.*"

"And you think that's a good thing?"

"If you have a problem with that, too bad. I knew I was better off on my own. I never should have agreed to let you be a partner."

Lindsay was unbelievable. She really did care about her work more than anything else. She made it almost impossible for anyone to get to know her, she was cranky in the morning and couldn't sleep without the hall light being on.

Why had he ever thought she might be the woman for him?

"The paperwork hasn't been signed," he reminded her. "Trust me, I'm not as keen about working here anymore, either."

"Good. We're agreed then. Our deal is off."

"Fine by me." His insides felt like they'd been scraped over concrete, but right now he was too proud and too angry to show it. "I'll clear out my office."

"And give me back my key."

"And give you back your key," he agreed, anger stiffening his lips. With long, deliberate strides, he made his way to the office he had occupied so briefly. It didn't take long to refill the cardboard box he'd recently unpacked and to slip his personal items into his briefcase.

All the while, Lindsay stood in the doorway, watching, arms crossed over her chest. He couldn't read her expression at all. He'd never seen her eyes so cold and angry.

When he was done, there was just one last matter to settle. "Keep the retainer for the Burchard case."

"We should split it. Fifty-fifty."

"You can go ahead and send me a check, but I won't cash it." He brushed past her, dropped his key on Nadine's desk, then headed for the door. He was just reaching for the handle, when she called to him.

"Nathan."

His shoulders tensed as he waited to hear what she would say.

"Did you buy that happy reconciliation story?"

Bloody hell. He supposed it had been too much to hope for an apology. "Not at all."

"Me, either. What do you think we should do about it?"

"You shouldn't do a thing. Leave it with me." And then he left.

LINDSAY TOLD HERSELF SHE WAS fine. Nathan was gone, but life would go on. Nadine returned to her desk and, without saying a word, resumed working.

Lindsay retreated to her office where she called the receptionist at the investment firm where Albert Walker-Smythe claimed to work.

Ignoring the knot that was tightening in her gut, she calmly asked if she could speak to Mr. Walker-Smythe.

"I'm sorry. I have no listing for someone with that name."

"You're certain Albert Walker-Smythe doesn't work there?"

"Positive."

One more lie from Albert Walker-Smythe. One more very good reason Carlene Schultz shouldn't marry him. The next thing she should do was—

Lindsay stared off into space. In her mind she could see Nathan's face as she'd told him that their brief affair had been a mistake. For one instant his eyes had clouded with pain.

And then, like her, he'd turned that pain into anger. And she'd been glad, because she'd rather deal with anger than pain any day.

If there was one lesson to learn from this, it was letting people get too close was always a mistake. The key to happiness was maintaining your distance. Focus on helping others.

People like Carlene Schultz.

If not for her, Carlene would be marrying this lying cheat one week from now. At some point in the future— maybe a week, maybe a year—Carlene would have been brokenhearted and considerably poorer than she was right now.

Lindsay was going to save her from that fate. She turned to her keyboard and started typing the report. When she was finished, she dialed Carlene's number. "This is Lindsay Fox from Fox Investigations."

"Boy, you are fast. I didn't expect to hear from you so soon." Carlene sounded nervous. Hopeful, but nervous.

Over the line Lindsay heard a door close, then Carlene spoke again.

"Okay. We can talk now."

"Good. I've completed my preliminary background check, Carlene, and I'm sorry to tell you that some of the information your fiancé told you about himself isn't true."

"No?" Carlene sounded deflated.

"He didn't graduate from the University of Florida, or any of the other major universities or colleges in that area. Nor is he employed at the brokerage firm you mentioned."

"Maybe I didn't get the names right. Maybe—"

"There's one more important fact I have to tell you. Your fiancé has a criminal record. He served two years for mail fraud and filing false statements."

"Oh." There was a long pause. "Are you sure?"

"I am." Since Carlene had been able to provide her fiancé's birth date and social security number there was no doubt they were talking about the same man.

"I don't suppose—" She fell silent, unable to complete the thought. Or maybe she was recognizing her empty hopes for exactly what they were.

"I'm sorry I didn't have better news." Lindsay didn't enjoy bursting her client's hopes and dreams for the future. This was, in fact, one of the hardest parts of her job. "I know it feels awful right now…"

She thought of Nathan, of the terrible knot in her stomach that wasn't going away, despite her rationalizing. "But you're better to find out this stuff sooner than later."

"You're right. It feels awful."

"I'll send you my written report in the mail. Please call me if you have any questions once you receive it."

After she'd said goodbye and hung up the phone, Lindsay stared at the redbrick wall of the neighboring building. There was plenty of work to be done, but an unaccustomed lethargy kept her glued in place.

Where had Nathan gone after he'd left her office? What would he do now? Would she ever see him again?

The phone rang and she was glad for the contact from the outside world. Soon she was busy on a missing persons case and several hours passed without her thinking about Nathan, though her stomach never stopped hurting.

Around four o'clock, she started thinking about the meeting with Celia that morning. Was it possible Maurice Burchard had changed his mind and wanted back in the marriage?

Had Audrey intended to kill her husband? Did she know about Paige Stevens? Was she really willing to resume a marriage that had fallen so publicly off the rails?

So many unanswered questions. Worst of all was a nagging suspicion that she was only seeing part of the picture. That a plan was in the works and someone innocent was going to be hurt.

She thought of Nathan, and wondered if he felt the same way. But there was no way she could consult with him now. She had to make her own plans. She'd been pulled off the case by the daughter, but on her own time she wouldn't mind checking on Maurice. If he was serious about reconciling with Audrey, then he should have cut his ties with the mistress. She'd like to make sure that he had.

Lindsay grabbed her leather case, then left her office. Nadine was at the open filing cabinet and she looked up with an expression of wariness.

"Are you okay?" she asked tentatively.

"I'm fine. I'm going to be out of the office for the rest of the afternoon. You can close up early if you feel like it." She hesitated, then added, "I know it's been a difficult day."

"Um…Lindsay?"

She already had her hand on the door. She inhaled deeply, then masked her impatience with a tight smile. "Yes?"

Her receptionist was definitely looking nervous now. Lindsay cast her eyes around the room, trying to spot something new. "What is it? Did you buy another plant?"

"I realize my timing isn't great, but it's month-end on Friday and there's something I really need to tell you."

Lindsay dropped her hand, resigned to a longer delay than she'd expected. "This sounds serious."

"It—it sort of is. Well, I didn't think it was, but Nathan—"

This involved Nathan? Lindsay moved closer. She could see the younger woman's hand trembling as she pushed the filing cabinet door shut.

"...well, he thought I should tell you the truth."

"The truth would be good."

"You see, my name isn't really Nadine Kimble."

CHAPTER FIFTEEN

LINDSAY WASN'T OFTEN SHOCKED, but this qualified as one of those times. "Impossible," she said after Nadine's statement had sunk in. "I checked your references and your background myself."

"Actually, you checked my cousin Ashley's background. Her mom is my mom's sister. Ashley's full name is Ashley Nadine Kimble. Nadine is our grandmother's name. Ashley and I are the same age and we went to the same schools."

Lindsay stared at her in disbelief. This still wasn't computing. "But why? Is there something in your past you needed to hide?"

"Just my last name." She mentioned a surname often sported in gossip magazines and on entertainment television.

Lindsay's eyes widened. "As in the Waverly hotel chain? Are you related to—"

Nadine didn't let her finish. "Yes. Madison is a cousin on my father's side of the family. When I tell people about the relationship, they get preconceptions."

No doubt. Madison Waverly had done it all. The wealthy socialite was on magazine covers, reality TV, sex tapes on the Internet. It seemed there was no limit to her desire for fame and attention.

"I wanted to start this job with no baggage, to be judged for myself and the work that I do."

Lindsay was speechless, at first. Nadine—*her* Nadine—was from one of the city's oldest, wealthiest families. No wonder she dressed so well.

She supposed she ought to ax Nadine on the spot for her deception. But, damn it, she liked Nadine. And Nadine was a fabulous receptionist. Besides…she was already down one employee for the day.

"Are you going to fire me?"

"I probably should. What you did wasn't exactly legal."

Nadine looked like a dog who had just been kicked.

"But, no. I'm not going to fire you. Not unless you start posting sex videos on the Internet." She thought about it for a moment. "Probably not even then."

"That's a big relief. Not the part about being able to post sex videos…" Nadine's face pinkened. "You know what I mean. Thank you, Lindsay. I love working here. Though, I am going to miss Nathan."

Just the mention of his name hurt. "Do me a favor and let's not talk about him for a while, okay?"

SOMETIMES WHEN SHE WAS working surveillance, Lindsay would borrow her sister's dog. It was a win/win situation. The little dust mop got an extra-long walk out of the deal, and she had a perfect cover. No one would ever be suspicious of a woman with a dog in Central Park.

After a quick meal of Vietnamese noodles, Lindsay went home to change into sweats, a ball cap and a large pair of sunglasses. Next she picked up Sadie from her sister's apartment, then headed to East Eighty-sixth Street, via the park. She recalled that there was a bench right across the street from Maurice's apartment building. Fortunately it happened to be empty.

She made herself comfortable, then offered Sadie one of those disgusting chewing treats—her sister called them pig's ears, but surely they weren't that—to keep her occupied for a while. Then she opened the paper she'd purchased on her way over and pretended to be engrossed in the daily catalog of murders, political blunders and celebrity gossip.

It was almost five and the streets were flooded with commuters on their way home from the office. Every few minutes someone new would enter the apartment building, stopping to converse with the doorman before proceeding inside. She watched a young mother, holding on to her preschool daughter with one hand, and juggling a bag of groceries and an oversize purse with the other.

A few minutes later a middle-age man hurried up the steps carrying a bottle in a brown paper bag.

Lindsay kept a careful eye on all the activity, while at the same time managing to occasionally turn a page of her paper or offer a pat for Sadie. As the sky darkened, she began to feel chilled. She zipped up her jacket, then slipped a red sweater over Sadie's head and front legs.

The poor dog looked totally miserable in her cute doggy outfit. "I'm sorry, Sadie. Meg made me promise."

Lindsay wondered how much longer she should sit here and wait. Soon it would be dark and there was no telling when Paige Stevens might come home. Meg would worry if she didn't bring Sadie back soon.

A tall kid wearing a hoodie and jeans with the crotch

hanging almost at his knees, skateboarded by. Though he appeared to have his board under control, Lindsay thought he was moving much too fast to be safe. She tightened her hold on Sadie's leash. "Slow down, buddy," she called after the kid.

About five minutes later the skateboarder circled back. Seeing him approach, Lindsay pulled Sadie close again. The kid had his head tucked down and seemed to be headed straight for her. When he was only a few feet away, he shifted his weight to the back of the board and braked to a crawl.

Great. She'd probably pissed him off and now she was going to get into a stupid, and potentially violent, confrontation. She didn't doubt that she could handle the situation, but she was on a job here. She wasn't supposed to be drawing attention to herself.

"Hey, Fox," the skateboarder kid said. "Nice disguise, but I think mine is better. The dog is a cute touch, though."

Holy cow, the skateboarder was Fisher. Lindsay felt a flooding of emotion—everything from illogical happiness to downright annoyance.

"You look about sixteen years old," she said.

"I'll take that as a compliment." He leaned over to pet Sadie. "Your sister's dog?"

"Yeah. Sadie, this is Nathan Fisher. Keep your distance, he's a dangerous dude."

Their eyes met for a long moment. She couldn't see a trace of Nathan's usual warmth or humor. His anger had cooled, but it had also hardened. A wedge lay between them now. And she had placed it there.

It's better this way, she reminded herself, trying to

keep her emotions calm and collected as he settled on the bench beside her.

She didn't need to ask what Nathan was doing here. Same thing as her, obviously. "I've been watching for over an hour," she told him. "No sign of Paige or Maurice."

"The penthouse is dark," Nathan observed. "One of them has to come home sooner or later." He stretched out his legs, as if he intended to stay until it happened.

"Unless Maurice was sincere about the reconciliation."

"In which case when Paige comes home, she'll be alone. Not that that will prove anything conclusively. But it might make me a tiny bit more inclined to believe the story Maurice is feeding his wife and his daughter."

Lindsay nodded. She shared Nathan's cynicism about the reconciliation. After witnessing Maurice and Paige together the other night, how could she not?

"If he doesn't honestly want to save his marriage, what do you think Maurice is up to?"

"No idea," Nathan admitted. "Do you have any theories?"

"None that don't sound half-baked."

"Yeah. I've got a few of those, myself."

This is good, Lindsay told herself. *We're talking about work and everything is civil.*

But it wasn't easy to focus with Nathan sitting so close. Her thoughts kept circling back to the weekend, to the somewhat amazing fact that only twelve hours ago they'd been cuddled in bed together.

What a mistake that had been.

Nathan checked the time on his watch. "Past six.

It's getting cool. No sense both of us sitting here hungry and cold."

"You go. I'll let you know if I see them."

"Technically you shouldn't even be here," Nathan said. "Celia did pull you off the case this morning."

"She pulled *us* off the case."

"I'm not here in an official capacity, but as a concerned friend of the family."

Did he mean to taunt her by reminding her of his former relationship with Celia? If so—it was working. Lindsay didn't try to hide her annoyance. "I may not be a friend of the family, but the contract we signed had Fox Investigations on the letterhead and my signature at the bottom. That made Celia *my* client, and I happen to care about my clients. Even when they stop sending me checks."

Nathan seemed surprised by her outburst. Then he sighed. "I know you care. It's why you're so good at what you do. But have you ever thought that maybe you care too much about some things, and not enough about others?"

"Damn it, Nathan. We set ground rules to our relationship—there were no promises."

"You set up those rules. I didn't. Excuse me for having normal, human emotions for the women I sleep with."

"Are you saying my emotions aren't normal?"

His jaw tightened, then he spit out, "Emotions? What emotions? Unless you're talking about anger. That's one emotion you seem to have mastered."

She was struggling to think up a scathing response when she noticed a familiar redhead on the sidewalk across the street. Paige Stevens was wearing a trench coat unbuttoned over a navy business suit. Probably on her way home from work.

Nathan had spotted her, too. Silently they watched as she waited for the doorman to allow her entry. About two minutes later bright lights flooded the upper floor of the building.

"So where's Maurice?" Lindsay wondered. "Is it possible the affair is over?"

"Maybe." Nathan stood and balanced one foot on the skateboard. "Seems to be a lot of that going around." Then he pushed off and rolled down the path until he was out of sight.

NATHAN CROSSED THE STREET to a coffee shop. He'd be able to keep an eye on the apartment building from here, for a while at least, without arousing suspicion. He tucked his board under one arm then went up to the counter and ordered a large green tea and a blueberry oat muffin.

A counter with stools along the window wall provided a handy spot for him to sit and watch.

Only the first spot he checked wasn't the apartment building next door, but the park bench across the street. It was empty. He scanned the surrounding area but could see no sign of Lindsay and her sister's little bichon.

Well. That was a good thing, he told himself.

He cupped his cold hands around the mug of tea. More warmth here than he'd ever felt from Lindsay. Of all the women to be attracted to. He should count himself lucky it had ended as quickly as it had.

From this seat he had a perfect view of the apartment's front entrance. If Maurice showed up to meet his lover, Nathan would spot him for sure. Every fifteen minutes or so someone either entered or left the building. But it was never Paige leaving or Maurice arriving.

Once his tea and muffin were gone, Nathan called his sister.

"What's up? We hardly saw you this weekend."

"Just a job," he said, sorry for the lie but unable to talk about Lindsay just yet. "How are you and Justin doing?"

"Great. We went to visit June Stone on Sunday—remember me telling you about her?"

"Of course, I do."

"Well, the apartment is wonderful. And there's a park for Justin across the street."

"So you think you're going to move?" He'd miss his sister and Justin. Which only made him realize that it was time he got his own personal life in order.

"At the end of next month."

"I'll help," he promised. By then he'd be completely unemployed, with lots of free time on his hands. But he wouldn't worry Mary-Beth with that news, yet. Not until he'd decided what to do.

He could always go back to the police force—Lt. Rock had made that very clear. Alternatively, he could go into business for himself, as Lindsay had done. There were advantages to each, though right now, he couldn't muster much enthusiasm for either option.

LINDSAY LOOKED OVER THE RIM of her third paralyzer and sighed. Would this crazy day never end? Her sister had just walked into the Stool Pigeon dressed in tall boots and a trench coat that probably covered her pajamas. Meg was usually in bed by ten and it was almost midnight now.

It took Meg a while to find her amid the smattering of other regulars sitting at tables and along the bar. Lindsay didn't make it easy for her by waving or calling out. Instead, she slunk into her booth seat and tried looking inconspicuous. Her sister didn't belong here.

Wendy approached with a tray full of empty glasses. Lindsay glowered at her. "You called Meg, didn't you?"

Wendy just shrugged.

There was something to be said for patronizing a bar where no one knew your name. Or your sister's name, for that matter.

"There you are." Meg had finally spotted her. She walked up to the booth, slid onto the opposite bench seat, then proceeded to examine her older sister as if she was an uncooperative witness.

"This is my place," Lindsay said finally. "My hangout. Not yours. Why aren't you in bed? Or should I say, *still* in bed?" She'd been right about the pajamas. She could see a bit of blue flannel above the top button of Meg's trench.

Noticing her gaze, Meg pulled her coat tighter. "I'm here because I'm worried about you."

"No need for that. Go home and get your beauty rest. You know how grouchy you are if you don't get your eight hours."

Predictably, Meg ignored her advice. She leaned closer. "I assume this has something to do with Nathan?"

Bingo on the first try. Her sister always had been the bright one. "How's Sadie? I hope I didn't tire her out too much tonight. Thanks again for letting me borrow her. She made an excellent cover."

"She's fine. She loved the long walk. She'll probably sleep until noon tomorrow. Now tell me about Nathan."

"Would you please stop mentioning that name?" Lindsay tried signaling Wendy for another drink, but the wretched woman pointedly ignored her. Lindsay set her empty glass to the side with the other two. Apparently Wendy was clearing every glass in the place tonight, except hers. As if Lindsay couldn't keep track of how many drinks she was having.

Meg was eyeing those empty glasses now, her expression worried. "This isn't good."

"I don't drink to be good. I drink to *feel* good." No. That wasn't true, either. She drank so she wouldn't feel. Tonight the numbness was elusive.

Wendy ambled up to them. Business was slow this time of night and she didn't move very fast at the best of times. She placed two empty mugs and a pot of tea on their table, then fixed her gaze on Lindsay as if daring her to complain.

Lindsay took a sniff, then wrinkled her nose. "Chamomile?"

"Perfect. Thanks, Wendy." Meg poured the brew into the mugs then pushed one toward Lindsay.

"Talk some sense into your sister. We thought she was finally getting a life. Now this." Wendy shook her head despairingly, before heading to the front of the bar to clear a recently vacated table.

Meg folded her arms on the table and leaned even closer. "He seemed like a nice guy. What happened?"

Reminding herself that her sister's intentions were

good, Lindsay capitulated. "Fine. If you must know, we spent the entire weekend together."

Meg smiled. "And it was good?"

"*Very* good." Lindsay started to smile, too, but ended up sighing. "The trouble started this morning. One of our clients is an ex-girlfriend of Nathan's. She sensed the new relationship between us, and went crazy."

"Oh, dear."

"It was ugly, let me tell you. But I needed the shake-up. I realized I'd made the cardinal mistake of mixing business with pleasure."

"Don't tell me you broke up with him?"

"Of course I did."

"But you're still working together?"

"Definitely not. Meg, you should have been there. It was so unprofessional."

"Lindsay, for a smart woman, you can be so dense. People who work together have love affairs all the time. Sometimes they get married. I should tell you all the stuff that goes on in my office."

"So it goes on. That doesn't make it right."

"No. It makes it human. It's only natural that men and women are attracted to one another and that when they spend a lot of time together, sometimes they fall in love."

"I'm not in love. This thing with Nathan…it was supposed to be fun, without strings attached."

"If it was 'just sex' then why are you sitting alone in a bar, feeling miserable?"

"I'm not—" She stopped midway through her denial. Yes, she was miserable. This weekend, she'd actually been happy. Happier than she could ever remember feeling in her life.

"What's wrong with me? Why did I have to push him away?"

"Because your emotions were getting involved, and that scares you. It always has."

"Hell. You're right. What should I do? Do you think I should try therapy again?"

But she hated therapy. She'd certainly tried enough of it in the past.

"Maybe. Or you could try calling him. Apologizing."

Lindsay shook her head. "What would I apologize for? Being myself?"

She couldn't help the way she was. Just because she knew that her anger, her need to keep people at a distance, had been caused by the death of her parents, didn't change anything. She wanted to be different, but she simply wasn't.

"I told him the rules. If he wanted to be with me, he would have accepted them."

"Oh, Lord." Meg cupped her hands on either side of her head in a gesture of hopelessness. "Maybe you *should* try therapy again. Not that it's done that much for me. At least not as far as men go."

Meg was a powerhouse when it came to her job, dealing with clients and appearing in court. But put her in a social situation with a man and she was all nerves.

"We are such a mess," Lindsay said.

"At least I can sleep at night. And I don't need that." Meg pointed at the empty drink glasses, then pushed the cup of tea toward her sister. "Drink up. Then I'm walking you home."

When Lindsay tried to protest, her sister stayed firm. "Do it, Lindsay. Or you're never getting rid of me."

Lindsay sipped the chamomile tea, then made a face. "I suppose this is what they call tough love."

"That's what sisters are for."

DESPITE MEG'S GOOD INTENTIONS, the tea and a long hot soak in her tub, Lindsay couldn't sleep. At two in the morning she turned on her computer and checked her e-mail. She was surprised to see a message from Nathan. She quickly moved the curser to open it.

Lindsay, thought you'd like to know that when I left the stakeout at midnight tonight, Maurice still hadn't shown up. If you want to keep an eye on the place tomorrow, I'll cover Wednesday. Let me know if that works. Nathan.

CHAPTER SIXTEEN

LINDSAY READ NATHAN'S MESSAGE several times over. No matter how hard she tried, she couldn't see anything between the lines. Short, professional and blunt. Even his sign-off had been the bare minimum: his name.

She swiveled her chair away from the computer and gazed over her living room. She could still see signs of her weekend with Nathan. Two cups on one of her speakers. One of Nathan's navy socks stuck between the cushions on her sofa. She plucked it out and considered returning it to him. She tried to imagine what his sister would say if she rang their doorbell at two-thirty in the morning.

"I'm sorry to disturb you, but I thought Nathan might be missing this."

She laughed. And then she threw the sock across the room, or at least tried to. The sock was so light it landed like a feather just a few feet from where she was standing. She left it on the weathered hardwood floor.

Maybe she should make some more tea. But she didn't want tea. She thought of all the ingredients she had chilling in her fridge. The vodka, the tequila, the coffee liqueur.

But she'd promised Meg, no more tonight, and really

it was a promise she wanted to keep. Certain lines were just too dangerous to cross.

Lindsay went back to her computer and hit Reply.

Thanks for the update. I'll take care of Tuesday. I'll let you know how it goes. Lindsay.

She hit Send then turned on spider solitaire. Partway through the game her computer signaled an incoming message. Quickly, she switched screens, her heart racing at the sight of Nathan's name in her in-box, again.

She opened the message.

Sounds like a plan. But what are you doing up at this hour? Go to bed, Lindsay. Get some sleep.

What about you? she wanted to ask. *Why are you still awake so late?*

She smiled at his typical Nathan-like concern. But the warm feeling quickly faded into sorrow and pain. Like Meg said, he was a really good guy. Much too nice a person for someone like her.

TUESDAY, LINDSAY FELT LIKE HELL. Not enough sleep. Too much thinking about Nathan. A very bad combination.

It didn't help that she had to spend the day performing routine background checks for one of her corporate clients. The pay was good, the work was steady. But this was the sort of administrative brain workout someone like Nathan could do in half the time it took her.

Nadine wisely avoided her for most of the day, ensuring only that incoming calls were dealt with and the coffeepot remained full and fresh at all times.

At lunch Lindsay went out to grab a hot dog and a bit of air. She ordered a jumbo dog from a street vendor, loaded the bun with mustard, then took off down

Columbus Street, walking with no destination in mind, just to get a little exercise.

Within two blocks she'd finished her hot dog. She was about to turn around when she noticed someone familiar sitting at the window of the Garden Café. He had his back to her, but she recognized his hair, his jacket, the set of his shoulders.

She moved closer, wondering who Nathan was having lunch with. The restaurant was the kind he would like, specializing in all sorts of healthy, vegetarian fare. It was fronted with large glass panes...the kind that opened to create the feel of a patio in nice weather. With today's cool temperatures, the windows were closed, but she could still see clearly inside.

Nathan was sitting at a table for two, and across from him was a tall, big man, with a round head and rough features.

She could tell, just from the way he held himself, that he was a cop. At second glance she realized Lt. Rock had been her and Nathan's superior officer.

She didn't have to be Sherlock Holmes to figure out the purpose of the meeting. The lieutenant was too senior to be Nathan's friend. This was a business meeting. Nathan was thinking of returning to the NYPD.

Lindsay wanted to pound her fist against the window. How could Nathan even talk to them after how he'd been treated? He was too good for them. He deserved so much better.

Someone jostled into her and Lindsay realized she was blocking traffic. What was she doing here, anyway?

It wasn't her business and she shouldn't care.

But she did.

HER QUIET OFFICE WAS THE perfect retreat for Lindsay that afternoon. She tackled the remaining background checks with grim determination, accepting it as her penance for screwing things up so badly with Nathan. By the end of the day, she had her report finished and an invoice printed and ready to be mailed to the client.

She handed both to Nadine with instructions for delivery. "You can leave once you've delivered these to the courier." She paused, slightly disconcerted by the knowledge that she'd just given such menial tasks to an heiress—someone who had no need of the monthly paycheck she was earning here.

"You could do anything. Be anyone. Why this? Why here?"

Nadine turned her hands, palms up. "I don't know how to explain. I love that we're doing something *real*. Working for you, I feel alive in a way I've never felt before."

Lindsay glanced around the office, trying to imagine how Nadine must see it. "I know I'm not the easiest boss. And you've made it clear that you find these offices too sterile."

"I live in houses decorated by the world's best interior designers. I don't care about the decor. You hired me without knowing my background or my family. You hired me for myself. And besides…I've always loved books and movies about private investigators." She smiled sheepishly.

"It's not as exciting and glamorous as you expected, right?"

"Maybe not. But in a good way. You actually help people. Like Carlene Schultz. It would have been terrible if she'd believed everything that man told her and gone ahead and married him."

"There are rewarding moments. But sometimes the work is dull."

"I guess it must be that way in any profession. But I'm never bored. Though...I would like to learn more about the investigation side of the business. Once I've mastered reception," she added quickly.

Lindsay tried to imagine her petite, softhearted receptionist as an investigator. "Eventually, sure. On-the-job training is the best way to go, though maybe six months from now you'll be ready to enroll in some classes."

"That would be great. One more thing...is Nathan really gone for good?"

Lindsay felt the muscles in her neck and back stiffen. "Yes. We'll need to place our ad again." She hated the prospect of interviewing more job applicants. But the cases were still mounting.

"I'll take care of it first thing in the morning," Nadine promised, her tone lackluster. Lindsay understood. Nathan was not going to be easy to replace.

She left the office with a final wave at Nadine, then headed to her apartment to change into a jogging outfit. She might as well get a little exercise tonight as she kept an eye out for Paige and Maurice.

ON THURSDAY NIGHT NATHAN considered staying home with Mary-Beth and Justin. Mary-Beth had picked up a pumpkin at the market and they were planning on carving it tonight. She'd have her hands full with Justin running around the house in the teddy bear costume she'd made for him. He was so excited about the Halloween party at the day care tomorrow. He was too young to fully understand the holiday, but he knew it involved candy and that was enough to get him revved up. Mary-Beth was pretty restrictive when it came to sugary treats.

Nathan headed to the kitchen. The pumpkin was on the table and Justin had been strapped into his high chair. The pumpkin had been decapitated and eviscerated, the pulpy mass piled on the remains of Wednesday's *Times*. Mary-Beth had a black marker in her hand and was studying the pumpkin, critically.

"It's lopsided," she complained to her brother.

Nathan rotated the gourd about forty-five degrees.

"That's a bit better." She wrinkled her nose. "I can't decide what the face should look like. I don't want it to be scary."

"May I?" When his sister nodded, Nathan took the marker then outlined big, happy eyes and a goofy grin.

"Perfect." Mary-Beth took his sharpest carving knife and pierced the thick outer skin. "How about rinsing off the pumpkin seeds? We can toss them with salt and oil and roast them in the oven."

Nathan remembered their mother doing that. She had always taken care of the seeds, while their father helped him and his sister carve the pumpkin.

"I'd love to, sis, but I've got a job I should take care of. Even though it's probably a waste of time."

This morning he'd received an e-mail from Lindsay telling him that she'd seen no sign of Maurice at the penthouse last night. That made three nights in a row that Paige Stevens had returned home alone after work. It seemed unlikely that Maurice would show up today, just one night before his planned weekend away with his estranged wife. Still, for the sake of thoroughness, Nathan knew he had to make sure.

"I figured there had to be a reason you were dressed like that again." She eyed his skateboarding getup with a rueful shake of her head. "You'll be careful?"

He rarely provided details about his work, but he knew she worried. "It's just routine surveillance," he assured her. "The biggest risk is falling off my skateboard."

He leaned over to give his nephew a high-five. "See you later, buddy." With a final smile for his sister, he grabbed his skateboard and left.

NATHAN WAS COLD. AND TIRED. It was too dark to skate-board anymore, and he was back at the coffee shop, nurs-ing his second large green tea of the evening. This was the first night Paige Stevens hadn't returned home shortly after work. She could be out doing many things... dinner with friends, shopping, an after-hours meeting with a client.

But he had to hang around until she came home to be certain she wasn't with Maurice.

At ten o'clock, he was glad he'd waited. She stepped out of a taxi followed by none other than Celia's father. They didn't look like a couple that was breaking up, he mused, as they stopped for a kiss on the steps of the building.

Nathan abandoned his cup of tea on the counter and hurried outside. Staying in the shadows, he adjusted the zoom on his camera. Thankfully the apartment building had bright lights around the door. He shot off several photos, catching the end of the kiss, then the couple, arms entwined, entering the building.

Disappointed to have his hunch confirmed, yet not surprised, Nathan exchanged his camera for his cell phone. He had some trepidation about speaking to Lindsay in person. The remote e-mails they'd been exchanging this week were a much safer mode of communication.

But he wanted her to know this as soon as possible.

Lindsay answered on the second ring. "Did Maurice show up?"

Despite the lack of social niceties, his gut tightened at the sound of her voice. Nathan watched the lights on the upper story flash on. "They're inside right now."

"Well…so much for Maurice's noble intentions toward his wife and their marriage."

In her voice he heard the same emotion he himself had experienced. A tired resignation at having been proven right.

"I'll call Celia," he offered.

She hesitated a second, then said, "That's probably best."

And then she hung up. Just like that. Nathan glanced at the phone a second, then shook his head. What in the hell had he expected? An invitation to join her at the Stool Pigeon for a drink? Judging from the background noise, that was where she'd been when he called her.

Nathan pocketed his phone and considered his options. To go home he'd need to catch the subway. There was a stop near the Guggenheim. He started to head for it, but noticed a taxi with the light on headed his way. He raised his hand, and when the driver pulled over, he hurried inside.

"West Seventy-ninth and Columbus."

As the driver swung onto the Transverse Road through Central Park, the world seemed to darken. Cocooned in the backseat Nathan dialed Celia.

"Sorry to phone so late."

"It's okay, Nathan. I'm glad to hear from you."

Her voice was soft and honeyed and he realized she might be making the wrong assumption about this call. "I have something important to tell you about your father."

"My father?" Her tone sharpened. "I can't talk here. I'm at a party. Hang on a moment."

He heard background noises, footsteps, then a door closing. When Celia spoke again from the reverberation of her voice he guessed she had sought sanctuary in a restroom.

"Nathan, what are you talking about? I told you to leave my dad alone."

"Consider this a favor from a friend. I thought you should know that your father just went up to that penthouse apartment with his lover. Do you know if your mother is still planning to join him for the weekend?"

"Yes, she is. And so what if he's meeting with that nasty redhead? He's probably telling her that the affair is over."

Nathan pulled out his camera and reviewed the pictures. "Didn't look that way to me. Do you want to see the photos?"

"You spied on my dad and took pictures, too?"

He couldn't understand her anger. "You're the one who hired me to do just that."

"I wanted you to help my mom. And the best thing for her is if she and Dad reconcile."

It would be the best thing for Celia, too, he realized.

She wanted nothing more than for her life to return to normal and this whole ugly mess to disappear. And here he was, bursting her bubble.

"I'm sorry. I wish I could agree that your Dad is sincere about the reconciliation, but I'm afraid it's some kind of trick. We need to warn your mother. If you want, I'll call her."

"Don't you dare talk to my mother. Don't talk to any of us. You are not on this case anymore. Remember that, Nathan."

For the second time that night a woman hung up on him. He glanced out the window. The cab was just pulling up to the Stool Pigeon now. At night the bar didn't look as old and run-down as it did during the day. Still, he didn't think anyone would mistake it for anything other than what it was—a neighborhood hangout.

He paid the driver, who accepted the generous tip as his due, then stepped out to the street. Time to face some more rejection. But before he did, he was going to call Audrey Burchard. Despite Celia's orders, he didn't feel he had a choice.

Audrey sounded distracted when she answered the phone, but her voice turned cheerful when she realized it was him.

"Nathan. How are you?"

"I'm fine thanks. I assume Celia told you Lindsay Fox and I are no longer working on your case?"

"She did."

"So I'm just calling as a friend, wondering how you're doing."

"That's so sweet. I'm fine. I'm continuing with my

regular therapy sessions, though it isn't helping. I still can't remember shooting Maurice. And speaking of Maurice, he's told me he's interested in a second chance."

"Celia mentioned something about that."

"We're going out to our lodge for the weekend to spend some time together. He's picking me up at six tomorrow."

"How do you feel about that?"

She sighed. "I'm not sure. I'd love to turn the clock back on this whole messy affair. But that's not really possible, is it?"

"You shouldn't go if you don't feel comfortable."

"But I owe it to him. And to Celia."

"Audrey." He hesitated, then decided he had no choice. "What if I told you that Maurice is having an affair?"

For a moment she was quiet. Then she sighed again. "I'm not surprised. I suspected as much."

"What will you do now?"

"It doesn't change anything. Not really."

"But—he's *cheating*."

"Righteous anger is fine for someone young, with their life in front of them. But I'm in my fifties, Nathan. Most of my life has been spent with this man. We have a child together."

"So you're still going to go with him tomorrow?"

"It may come to nothing…but yes. I'm still going to try." Her tone changed, became brighter. "Thank you so much for calling, Nathan. I'm still rather regretful that things didn't work out between you and Celia."

"We were never that serious about each other."

"No. I sensed that. And certainly when I saw you with your partner—Lindsay Fox, right?—I could see where your heart truly lay."

He groaned. "I was that obvious?"

She gave a murmur of sympathy. "Things not going well on that front?"

"That front is stone cold, actually."

"Well, don't give up. If anyone can thaw her out, it would be you. And please don't worry any more about me. I'm going to be just fine."

Nathan disconnected the call, disappointed that he hadn't been able to talk her out of spending the weekend with Maurice. Nothing about this situation felt right to him. And now he had to face Lindsay. He squared his shoulders, then opened the door to the Stool Pigeon.

CHAPTER SEVENTEEN

LINDSAY WAS INSIDE, ALL RIGHT, sitting at the bar, watching the World Series game. She had a drink on the counter and was munching on peanuts from a bowl on the bar. He ought to warn her about the bacterial content. Really, the only thing those nuts were good for were squirrels.

As Nathan stood there watching, an older guy, three seats from Lindsay spouted some abuse at the Yankees' pitcher. Lindsay promptly put him in his place.

God, he liked the woman's style.

She had her signature drink in front of her, the glass atypically full. Perhaps the peanuts were slowing her down. He approached with caution. With Lindsay you never knew what to expect.

"Bottom of the ninth?" he asked as he slid onto the stool next to hers.

She'd been too absorbed in the game to notice him until then. He felt her stiffen and her casual reply came a second too slow.

"Yeah, and it's not looking good."

"You're not cheering for the Dodgers?"

"Why would I? I'm a New York City girl."

Her tone, almost belligerent, told him he'd better back off. Any personal information he'd learned about her past—like the fact that she'd grown up in California—he was now to forget. Her boundaries were constricting again, tighter and tighter.

Wendy's husband, Mark, slid a glass of mineral water in front of him. Nathan stared at the man, bemused. Did this mean he was now considered a regular? Or was this tacit encouragement in his quest to win Lindsay's heart?

If so, it was coming too late. He'd officially resigned from that hopeless cause. Now all he wanted was to prevent a disastrous conclusion of the one case they had worked on together.

"I called Celia," he said.

Lindsay kept her gaze on the game. "Was she surprised to find out her dad was still playing around?"

"She didn't believe it."

"Did you get photos?"

"She refused to see them. I called Audrey, too, and told her about Paige. She didn't seem to care. She's still leaving with him tomorrow at six." He took a drink of mineral water. "I'm planning to follow them."

Lindsay turned away from the TV and eyed him with measured curiosity. "You have a car?"

"I'm going to rent one."

She twisted her glass, revealing a damp ring of condensation, which she wiped away with her thumb. He noticed she still hadn't taken a sip even though the ice cubes were now slivers. He touched the glass. "What's with this?"

"My sister's worried about me, so I agreed to stop drinking for a month." She shrugged as if it was no big deal.

"You're serious?"

"Doesn't it look like I am?"

What a woman. "You've decided to avoid alcohol for a month, so here you are sitting in a bar with your favorite alcoholic drink in front of you. You sure like to make things hard for yourself."

"Where else would I hang out? Anyway, back to the case. What do you think Maurice is planning?"

"I still don't know," he admitted.

"Maybe we're wrong to be suspicious of Maurice. Maybe we should be worried about Audrey shooting him again, which she may well do now that you've told her about his girlfriend."

"That's why I feel like I have to be there. If one of them got hurt, I couldn't live with that."

"Even though Celia pulled us off the case?"

"Even though."

"Count me in," she said.

"I didn't come here to issue an invitation."

"Don't play games with me, Nathan. You know I have a right to be in on this."

"Don't accuse me of playing games. That's your specialty."

Her eyes widened as she registered the anger behind his words. "Don't turn this personal."

"Sorry. I keep forgetting, don't I? It was just sex." Pissed off as he was, he had to concede that her limitations had never extended to her job. She'd busted her butt on the Burchard case. She did deserve to be in on the finish, if she wanted to be.

"If you're serious about coming, be ready at five. I'll pick you up outside the agency."

He put a five on the counter to cover his water and didn't linger to hear her response. He knew she'd show up.

NATHAN WAS SERIOUSLY ANGRY at her, but Lindsay didn't care. He'd agreed to take her along to the Catskills. That was the main thing. When it came to her cases, Lindsay needed to see them through to the finish. Work was one area where closure was possible.

She eyed her drink, so close she could almost smell it, then reached for a peanut instead. On the TV screen the Dodgers were in the process of turning a double play. She groaned as Jeter was tagged out at home plate. That made two out.

Almost no chance for a comeback now, yet she prayed for one. Not just for the Yankees' sake. She didn't want this game to end, didn't want to get up from this stool and drag her butt down the block to her apartment. Since she'd determined to stop drinking, sleep had become even more elusive.

The moment she tried to relax, thoughts of Nathan would pop into her head. She was so damn tired of thinking of him.

What right did he have to be so angry at her? She'd warned him from the beginning about her emotional limitations. Did he think a little loving, some good sex and companionship were going to change her into a different person?

No doubt she wouldn't be the way she was if her parents hadn't died the way they had. But it had happened. And it had left a mark, on both her and Meg, that neither time nor counseling was ever going to erase. The tragedy was something they had to deal with as best as they could. If Nathan couldn't accept that fundamental truth about her, then it was just as well that he'd gone running.

Conversation around her silenced as the Dodgers' pitcher wound up for a crucial pitch. "Strike three. And that's it, folks. The Dodgers win this one, five to nothing…" She tuned out the rest of what the announcer had to say.

Mark came to commiserate with her. "That was a heartbreaker. I hate to admit it, but Steve was right. Our pitcher stunk."

"Everyone has an off night," she replied, but her heart wasn't into defending the Yankees anymore. She watched Mark clear away her drink with a sense of despair and also pride. She'd made it through another day without a drink.

LINDSAY WAS READY AND WAITING at five o'clock when the gray rental sedan pulled up to the curb in front of her. She was pumped about the case, but trepidatious about spending time with Nathan. They were both too angry to be alone together for an indeterminate length of time.

"Good choice with the car," she said as she opened the passenger door. The color and model were so non-descript they'd be practically invisible on the freeway. She tossed her backpack into the rear seat, then buckled her safety belt.

"Looks boring, but it's got turbo power." Nathan checked the traffic for an opening. When he found it, the car shot forward, proving his comment.

He was talking about the car, but he could also be describing the way she intended their conversation to flow, as well. Last night she'd decided that the only way she was going to survive this assignment was to limit conversation strictly to the case at hand.

Now she also decided she better limit eye contact, too. Nathan was dressed in black jeans and a dark gray sweater. Like the vehicle he drove, his clothing had been chosen to blend in with his surroundings. It also happened to make him look sexy as hell.

She fixed her gaze forward. That was when she noticed two take-out coffees in the holders on the dash. She reached for the one on her side.

"Thanks," she said, taking a sip. Hot, creamy and sweet. Perfect.

"It's going to be a long night. I figured we'd need the caffeine."

He had an excuse not to look at her. Traffic was always crazy in the city, especially just before the weekend. But she found it hard not to look at him. Lindsay took another drink of coffee and shifted her attention to the store windows as they sped past. Many had been decorated for the holiday. She'd almost forgotten tonight was Halloween.

"Will your nephew be going out to trick-or-treat?"

"He's too young. His day care had a party, though. He was pretty excited about that."

They fell back into silence then. Was Nathan as uptight as she was about being alone together? If his tight grip on the steering wheel was any indication, the answer was yes.

Nathan cut through Central Park and headed north to the Burchard town house on Park Avenue. He parked half a block down, behind a large truck. It was twenty past five.

"You think he'll be early?" Lindsay didn't know if it was the caffeine or adrenaline, but she was pumped. She could hardly wait to get moving, and hopefully find some answers to this disturbing case.

"Probably not. But it's better to wait a little longer than risk missing them."

The cautious approach was typical Nathan, but Lindsay ended up being thankful for his prudence when Maurice drove up in a navy Mercedes coupe about fifteen minutes ahead of the scheduled time.

She and Nathan were still sipping their coffee, listening to the radio and avoiding conversation when she spotted him.

He must have called ahead to warn Audrey that he'd be early, because she met him at the door with her suitcase. The silver-haired woman was dressed in classic Ralph Lauren cords, sweater and scarf for her weekend in the country. Using her binoculars, Lindsay zeroed in on her face. It seemed to her that the older woman looked nervous, but a little hopeful, too.

The couple pecked one another's cheeks, then Maurice carried his estranged wife's suitcase to the car and placed it in the trunk. Celia came to the door then. She gave both her parents tight hugs and watched from the doorway as they drove off.

Nathan waited, his fingers poised over the key in the ignition.

"Get going," Lindsay urged.

"I can't risk Celia recognizing us," he replied calmly. "Besides, I know where they're going. If we lose them, it won't be for long."

Eventually Celia returned inside, and Nathan was

able to drive past the town house and begin following the Mercedes. Within two blocks they had caught up to the navy coupe, weaving through traffic ahead of them. As Nathan had said, it did help knowing Maurice's ultimate destination. When they lost them at a red light, all Nathan needed to do was up his speed until he caught them again.

Eventually they were over the bridge and on the freeway heading north. City gave way to rolling mountains. The foliage was past its prime but still provided colorful jolts of red and yellow amid the green conifers. Autumn in New York was a much prettier season than it had been in California. Lindsay wished she could focus on the scenery for the entire trip but it was already growing dark.

"I wonder what Paige Stevens is doing this weekend?" Nathan said.

"We'll soon know if she's at home. I asked Nadine to keep watch on the penthouse this evening."

"Nadine?" Nathan looked surprised.

"Apparently she wants to try her hand at the investigating side of the business. I thought this assignment would give her a taste for the work."

"Poor thing. Did you prepare her for the boredom?"

Lindsay smiled. Surveillance was paradoxically the most exciting and the most tedious of an investigator's jobs. Tonight Nadine would definitely be experiencing only the tedium. She wouldn't have given her the assignment if there was any other possibility.

"I told her Paige usually comes home from work between six and seven. Nadine is going to call as soon as she does." Lindsay pulled out her cell phone to make sure it was on. The time displayed was 6:59 p.m. "We should hear from her anytime now."

As IT TURNED OUT, NADINE didn't get a chance to call Lindsay, because Lindsay phoned her first. It was almost midnight and she and Nathan were parked off the road in a copse of hemlock, surrounded by undergrowth that successfully concealed their location, a stone's throw from Maurice's parked Mercedes.

The Burchards' lodge was about five hundred yards off Route 296. To the north of the main building was a small guest lodge. Nathan had expected it to be empty. He'd even speculated that the two of them might break inside and pass the night there.

That was before Paige Stevens showed up.

With Nathan sitting silently beside her, Lindsay dialed the number of Nadine's cell phone. As soon as she answered, Nadine starting gushing.

"Lindsay, I'm so sorry. She still hasn't shown up. I don't think I missed her but maybe I did. At one point I almost fell asleep. And I'm awful at blending in with my surroundings, like you said I should do. So many people have stopped to ask if I need help or something. And it's cold! And I need to go to the bathroom! I don't know why I thought I'd be any good as an investigator. I'm doing a terrible job."

"Hang on, Nadine." It had been a tense evening, but Lindsay couldn't resist smiling now. Thanks to a full moon, there was enough light in the car that Nathan noticed. He raised his eyebrows questioningly, but she held a hand up for him to wait.

"You aren't doing a terrible job. You didn't see Paige

because she didn't go home. She drove up in a rented van about fifteen minutes ago."

Just before turning off the main road, the redhead had dimmed her headlights, then coasted to a parking space tucked behind the guest cottage. At the time Lindsay and Nathan had been outside, trying to see if they could break into the cottage without causing any damage, but all of the doors and windows were securely locked.

Nathan had pulled her back into the woods and they'd watched from their hiding spot as Paige used a key to let herself inside. Since then she hadn't given any sign of her presence. The guest cottage remained dark and silent, just like the main lodge.

"Paige Stevens is at the Burchards' Catskills lodge?" Nadine sounded confused. "But why?"

"I'm not sure. She had a key for the guest cottage. Maybe Maurice gave it to her. It's a safe bet Audrey doesn't know she's here."

"Is Audrey okay?"

"So far. It looks like she and Maurice are sleeping in separate bedrooms. Both lights went out about an hour ago."

"That doesn't sound like a very successful reconciliation."

"It doesn't, does it? Anyway, you can go home now, Nadine. I'm sorry you had such a long, boring night." She ended the call and powered off her phone. "That may be the end of Nadine's private investigator aspirations."

"I wouldn't discount her that quickly." Nathan's voice was low and deep in the silent night.

She felt a shiver that had nothing to do with the dropping temperature. Nathan had come prepared, with two blankets, a thermos of green tea, two paper cups and two bags of trail mix. They had to share nothing, except the vehicle.

She looked out at the full moon. In the deep, dark of the forest, it wasn't difficult to imagine witches and goblins on the prowl.

"You should get some sleep," Nathan said.

"Should we take turns?"

"I don't think anyone's going anywhere tonight. How about I set my watch alarm for dawn?"

"Okay." She reclined her seat and pulled the blanket to her chin. The warmth was unsatisfactory when all she could remember was the way it had felt to press her body next to Nathan's and to feel his arms holding her close.

Whatever had changed between them, the sexual attraction remained strong. She thought he must feel it, too, the huge awareness of how few inches stood between his arm and hers.

Rather than stare longingly at his profile, she forced her gaze upward. The car had a sunroof and she could see the shadowy darkness of overhanging branches and way beyond those, flirting glimpses of the star-filled sky.

Although she'd only caught three or four hours of sleep last night, she felt wide-awake. Nathan's breathing was slow and even. God, she envied his ability to drop off anytime, anywhere.

Suddenly hungry, she reached for the package of trail mix. As she attempted to open the cellophane package quietly, she felt like a coughing theater patron, trying to discreetly unwrap a throat lozenge. It seemed the quieter she tried to be, the more noise she made.

"Just open the damn bag, already," Nathan growled.

"Sorry." She quickly helped herself to a handful of mix, then set the bag on the dash. As she munched on the nuts and dried fruit, the sound seemed impossibly loud. Nathan must have also found it loud. He sighed, then shifted in his seat.

Lindsay swallowed, then stared out the sunroof again. So much for eating. She'd have to find some other way to pass the hours until dawn.

"Can't sleep?"

She shifted in the seat that had once seemed so comfortable. "I'll take that as a rhetorical question."

A moment passed, then Nathan asked, "Why do you think Paige is here?"

She'd been wondering the same thing. Also one other thing. "Do you think Maurice knows she's there?"

"He must. She has a key."

"Maybe she still has it from another visit."

"Maybe. But my hunch is that Maurice and Paige are planning to confront Audrey together in the morning."

"To what extent and to what purpose?"

"Maybe asking for a quick and easy divorce? Who knows...we'll have to wait and see."

She fidgeted with her watch strap. Waiting was not her strong suit.

They discussed certain possibilities and outlined plans of action for each one. Eventually their conversation dwindled. Nathan yawned. She guessed he would fall asleep in a minute flat if she stopped talking.

"So you're planning to go back to police work?" As

soon as she'd asked the question, she wanted to reel it back in. They'd been doing so well. Focusing on the job and ignoring everything personal—including the fact that all either of them had to do was reach out a hand and they'd be touching.

"Sorry," she added quickly. "That isn't my business."

"No, it isn't. So why do you know anything about it?" With a quick snap, Nathan had his seat in the upright position again.

"I happened to see you having lunch with Lt. Rock."

"At the Garden Cafe?"

"Yes. Nathan, how could you even consider going back after what they put you through?"

"What's it to you? You made it pretty clear you don't give a damn about me."

"No. I made it clear that I didn't *want* to give a damn about you. It's not the same thing."

Expecting a quick retort, she was confused by silence. Nathan seemed to be thinking about what she'd said. When he finally spoke again his tone was gentle.

"Are you saying you *do* care?"

"Of course, I care. That doesn't change anything. I'm still the same person. What did you call me—cold and remote? It's not something I can change." She was a bad risk for the long haul. And a guy like Nathan, well, before long he'd find someone sweet and loving who had no shadows hanging over her bed late at night.

"Lindsay, you drive me crazy. Nothing's ever easy with you. Nothing."

"And it never will be. So thank your lucky stars you got out in time."

She shook her head and closed her eyes. Lindsay finally fell asleep about an hour before dawn. He was struck again by how innocent and young she looked when she was sleeping. He wished that once she surrendered in sleep she would just plunge back into her old...

CHAPTER EIGHTEEN

NATHAN DID NOT CONSIDER himself lucky. Lindsay could think he'd gotten out of their relationship free and clear, but he knew better. Even with his eyes closed, every nerve in his body was tuned in to her presence beside him. All his instincts were urging him to touch her, to pull her closer, to kiss her.

It didn't seem to matter that she encouraged none of this. She'd pushed him away, and he'd left her and had felt terrible as a result. Now that he was with her again—even in this uneasy state of truce—he finally felt alive.

He loved her.

With considerable effort, he sat still in his seat, resting, feigning sleep, waiting to hear the elusive sound of Lindsay's gentle snoring. Beside him she was a bundle of potential energy. Though she sat relatively still, he could sense her restlessness. He let his mind wander and soon he was dozing. Next time he opened his eyes, the display on the dash said it was three-fifteen. He turned slightly and met the blue flash of Lindsay's gaze.

He felt a deep sympathy for her predicament, but knew better than to voice it. "Want to listen to the radio for a while?" he offered.

She shook her head and closed her eyes. Lindsay finally fell asleep about an hour before dawn. He was struck again by how innocent and young she looked when she was sleeping. He resisted the urge to touch her face, settling instead for pulling her blanket up to her chin.

THE BEEPING OF NATHAN'S WATCH woke Lindsay just as she was settling into deep REM sleep. She opened her eyes, foggy-brained and disoriented.

Next to her, Nathan was already awake. His seat was upright, though he was still covered with the blanket. It was freezing in the car.

"Did something happen?"

"Not yet."

His gaze scanned warmly over her, and she automatically put a hand to her hair. She finger-combed the tangled strands, then ran her tongue over her teeth. "I could use a toothbrush."

"Try this." He handed her a stick of peppermint gum.

"Thanks." She tried to peer out one of the windows but they were covered in condensation. Using the edge of her blanket, she wiped off the passenger side. Outside she saw nothing but trees and underbrush. She edged open the door.

"Where are you going?"

"To use the facilities." She stepped out onto damp ground matted with spruce needles and dead leaves. She moved along the spongy surface, slipping between tree branches, deeper into the woods. When she could no longer see the car, she relieved herself, then used her travel bottle of hand sanitizer.

Light seeped out from the east, a colorless beginning to a cloudy day. She went still and listened carefully, but no sounds emerged from either the lodge or the guest cabin.

Back in the car, Nathan had set out a breakfast, of sorts. Tetra boxes of orange juice and cranberry granola bars. She ate because she needed to, forcing the food into a stomach that was churning with anticipation and nerves.

They had no idea what Maurice and Paige were up to. All they knew was that *something would* happen and they had to be prepared in case intervention was required. They both had their phones charged and in their pockets. Nathan turned the radio on quietly and they listened to a forecast that called for warmer temperatures and sunshine.

"Did you bring your gun?" Nathan asked at one point.

"No." The question alarmed her. She almost never took her gun out of the locked drawer where she kept it. "Did you?"

He shook his head in the negative. "I gave it up when I quit the force."

The minutes seemed to tick by interminably. Finally, after about an hour, they heard sounds from the lodge. Audrey called out something and Maurice replied, his voice a low mumble. Fifteen minutes later the smell of coffee wafted out into the woods.

Lindsay groaned quietly. Their mugs of take-out coffee were long gone and so was every last drop of the tea. She glanced at Nathan and knew he was longing for the same thing she was.

"We need to take our mind off the aroma of that coffee," she said.

"Sex might do it."

His suggestion made her feel instantly hot, a reaction she tried to downplay. "Very funny."

"Or how about this?" He pulled a bar of dark chocolate from his pocket. "Not as good as sex, but it has caffeine."

She accepted a hunk gratefully. "Now that they're awake, we need to move within sight of the lodge."

He nodded, then exited the vehicle quietly. She followed, fighting back the competitive urge to take the lead. He'd been here before, was familiar with the layout. This time it made sense for him go first.

He pushed his way through the trees and shrubbery, pausing after a few minutes for her to catch up, then removing the last square of chocolate from the foil wrappings. "Want this?"

Not able to resist, she held out her hand. "You thought of everything, didn't you?"

"I try to plan for every contingency. For instance, if one of us is bitten by a poisonous snake, I've got my first-aid kit in my backpack."

Just as he said that, something rustled in the underbrush. She grabbed for his arm.

"Probably a mouse," Nathan said.

"Good." She had no problem with mice.

"Although this is perfect habitat for copperheads," he added.

She hesitated, one foot poised in the air. "You're trying to scare me."

"It's a fact. Copperheads account for the highest percentage of venomous snake bites in New York State." Then without another word, he started moving forward again.

Her sporty black running shoes had seemed sturdy enough yesterday when she was dressing. Now she wished she'd worn her hiking boots. She scanned the undergrowth around them wondering what sort of creatures were concealed within.

"You okay?" Nathan had turned back to look at her.

She swallowed through her paralyzing fear, and chastised herself. What was she going to do? Give up and go back to the city because she was afraid of snakes?

She kept walking. Nathan nodded approvingly, then resumed picking out the trail.

The woods were moist and dank. It must have rained during the short stretch when she'd been sleeping, which was a good thing as nothing would have revealed their presence more quickly than the crunch of leaves and sticks under their feet.

After a few minutes they had gained enough ground to see the main lodge. The log building was built ranch-style with a decorative old wagon wheel out front and a wooden porch running the length of the east-facing wall. The morning sun shone warmly on the porch with its old-fashioned wicker furniture. Besides a table and four chairs, there was also a cushioned sofa and several footrests.

"Nice place."

"Looks rustic, but trust me, they have every convenience inside. Including a propane heater for the porch."

"That sounds nice," Lindsay said, trying not to shiver.

Nathan touched her arm. "Let's get a little closer."

Again she followed, until they reached a shed that appeared to be used for storing firewood. Just as she recognized the woodsy scent of burning hickory, Lindsay noticed a trail of smoke escaping from the lodge's stone chimney.

She hugged her chilled body and scoped the area. This was a good hiding spot. Through a thick screening of shrubbery, they had a view of the porch and also the main doors to the lodge and the guest cabin.

Nathan settled onto a large stump, obviously used as a chopping block, and patted the space beside him. "Might as well get comfortable. We may be here awhile."

She hesitated, but there wasn't another dry place to sit. After pulling out her binoculars, she joined him on the seat, then set about adjusting the focus knob. With the binoculars she could see the pattern on the cushions and the individual strands of the woven wicker. But there was nothing of interest going on yet.

"See anything?"

"Not much." She let the binoculars rest on her thighs, then gazed around at the woods, looking everywhere but the one place she didn't dare—at Nathan.

For as crazy as he made her feel, she had to admit that there was no one she'd rather have with her right now. They had more talking to do, once this was over.

She lowered her gaze to the ground, which was flat and packed with sawdust. No hiding spaces here for snakes, thank goodness. The woods were quiet at this time of the year. Most birds had migrated, though in the distance she could see a crow swooping arcs above the treetops before finally settling on a safe perch at the top of a gothic-looking spruce.

Despite the quiet surroundings, her heart was hammering against her chest—too fast and too loud. She could feel the sheen of sweat on her fingers as she picked up her binoculars for another look.

Beside her Nathan appeared calm and focused. Their awkward night together hadn't seemed to faze him. He leaned forward, forearms resting on his thighs, and squinted into the distance. "Is that…?"

"What?" She was immediately on edge, adjusting the binoculars, trying to figure out where to train them.

He tilted his head. "Is that *bacon* I smell?"

"Bacon?" She lowered the glasses and glared at him. "I thought you saw something *important*."

He returned her scowl with a relaxed grin. "Settle down, Fox. Odds are we'll have to wait until they're finished eating before anything happens. How about when we're done here we head into Hudson for some breakfast? I could really go for a three-egg omelet and about a gallon of fresh coffee."

"And hash browns," she added. "And fresh squeezed orange juice. Not that reconstituted crap in the b— Oh—look." She pointed in the direction of the guesthouse, then checked the view through the glasses.

Paige Stevens had just stepped out of the guesthouse. Her flamboyant hair had been tamed into a ponytail and she was wearing jeans and a dark sweater. More important, she had a shotgun in her hands.

"Holy crap, Fisher. What do you think she's doing?" Lindsay focused in on the shotgun.

Nathan was at her side, leaning in close as if he wanted a look, too. She passed him the glasses. "The original shotgun—the one Audrey supposedly used to shoot Maurice—would have been confiscated by the police," he said. "I wonder where she got that one?"

"Maybe it's new?"

Nathan crept forward on his knees, careful to remain hidden amid the branches, as he angled for a better view. "She's hiding the shotgun under the cushions on the sofa."

Lindsay swore. "What are they up to?" She inched beside him, putting a hand on his shoulder to steady herself. Having secreted the gun under the seat cushion, Paige was now creeping back to the guesthouse.

"Nathan, we've got to warn Audrey. Do you think we could get to the porch without being seen?"

"No way. The Burchards eat breakfast in the kitchen, which overlooks this shed. We can't see them because of the glare on the windows, but if we step out from these bushes, they'll definitely see us."

He pulled out his phone. "I have a number for the landline to the lodge. I'll call Audrey and warn her to get out of there."

As he dialed the number, the front door to the lodge opened. Audrey, carrying a tray with two mugs of coffee and a carafe, stepped out to the porch, her husband right behind her. They were both dressed casually in sweaters and jeans, and they were talking. Their words carried faintly through the trees.

"That was a delicious breakfast, Audrey, thanks." Maurice settled onto the sofa.

"Can we talk now?"

The phone inside the lodge started ringing. Both of them turned their heads.

"I'll go get that—" Audrey began.

Her husband put a hand on her arm. "Just leave it."

She hesitated then nodded. "Fine."

Nathan and Lindsay exchanged disappointed looks, then Nathan disconnected the call. They watched as Audrey poured coffee from the carafe into each of the cups then went to sit beside her husband on the sofa. He shifted more to the center. "Why don't you sit on the chair, dear? You'll have a better view. Look at the colors on those hills. I thought the leaves would be gone by now."

"We need to call the cops," Nathan whispered urgently into Lindsay's ear. "He's sitting right on top of the gun. He has to feel it."

"He already knew it would be there," Lindsay surmised.

Nathan dialed the number for emergency. "I'd like to report a domestic disturbance. Let them know that there is a gun on the premises." He provided directions from the main highway to the lodge and when he was done, he slipped the phone into his shirt pocket. "It'll be at least half an hour before they get here. But I don't see what else we can do."

"We need to move closer," Lindsay said. "Circle round and sneak up from the back."

"Lindsay, we don't have a gun. I'm not letting you get any closer than this."

"That gun isn't there for looks, Nathan. Maurice plans to use it. And I'm not going to sit here and watch him kill Audrey. So...do you have another plan or are you going to help me find a route to the back of the lodge?"

Nathan looked angry enough to fire bullets himself but in the end he just nodded curtly, then started to move. Lindsay hurried to keep up with him as he circled the back of the shed and into the thick shrubbery. They hiked as quickly as they dared, crouched low and careful to avoid any sticks or loose stones. They had to cut a wide circle to avoid being seen—which meant their progress was slow.

Lindsay realized her breathing was becoming too fast, too shallow. She forced herself to stop panicking. "Relax. You can handle this," she muttered to herself, even though she was far from certain that she could.

Real life private investigating was not like TV. She'd never encountered a situation requiring a gun in her private practice before and while she owned one, had never considered carrying it along when she was on a case.

Finally she and Nathan were behind the lodge. Thank goodness the Burchards had kept the property in its natural state so there was no open lawn, no manicured garden. The wild undergrowth continued right up to a dirt path that circled the house. She and Nathan crept along until they were at the south side of the property.

They both froze when Maurice started speaking again. "There's something I haven't told you, Audrey."

Lindsay gazed at Nathan, and waited, breathless. Was Maurice about to confess his affair? Dimly she recognized the fact that her upper arm hurt. She looked down to see that Nathan had taken a firm hold of it. She tried to shake him off, but he only held her tighter.

"Let go of me," she whispered angrily.

He put a finger to his lips for her to be quiet.

"That big commercial real estate project I did last year?" Maurice said. "It's a bust. I've lost all my money."

"What happened? Why didn't you tell me sooner?"

"What was the point? There was nothing you could do."

"I could have lent you some money."

"A man can't borrow money from his wife if he intends to divorce her."

There was a deep, painful silence. Then Audrey found her voice. "You didn't bring me here because you wanted a reconciliation."

"No. I'm sorry it has to end this way. But you see, I don't have a choice."

Maurice's voice was utterly devoid of affection. Lindsay's fear turned to dread. "We have to help Audrey," she whispered to Nathan.

"Maurice has a gun," Nathan reminded her. "We're not cops anymore. Officially we're trespassing. You could lose your license over this."

She didn't care about that, but Lindsay gave up arguing with him as Audrey began to speak again. "If you still want a divorce," her voice quavered, then grew strong again, "we didn't need to drive all this way to talk about it."

"You don't get it. What I'm trying to say is that I can't afford to divorce you."

"What are you suggesting then?" Audrey was silent a moment, then continued, her tone disapproving. "If you're thinking we can stay married but live separate lives, then you can forget about it. Have your lawyer call my—"

She stopped talking so abruptly that Lindsay was afraid for her. Had Maurice hurt her?

Again she strained against Nathan's hold, and this time he pulled her against his hard chest. She put out a hand to push him away, but froze at the sound of Audrey's voice.

"Who are you?" Audrey demanded angrily. "Maurice, who is this woman?"

Lindsay looked at Nathan. He mouthed, "Paige Stevens," and she nodded. The other woman must have left the guest cottage. Why now? Was this part of the plan?

"She's your mistress, isn't she?" Audrey's voice was turning hysterical. "Maurice? What is going on here? You're scaring me. And what are you doing with those cushions? What's back there?"

Lindsay couldn't stand it anymore. The police hadn't arrived, couldn't possibly arrive for at least fifteen more minutes. Right this second Maurice was reaching for the hidden gun, she was sure of it. She couldn't let this happen.

Using her hip as a pivot point, she executed a judo throw that unbalanced Nathan, breaking his hold on her, and landing him in the dirt. As soon as she was free, she started to run.

"Lindsay, stop!" Nathan hissed at her, scrambling to his feet.

"I can't."

She had no plan, but she knew that Maurice did and she was not going to let him execute it.

CHAPTER NINETEEN

AS SHE ROUNDED THE CORNER, the first person Lindsay saw was Paige Stevens. Maurice's lover was halfway between the guest cottage and the porch, where the Burchards had been taking their coffee. Audrey had left her chair and was now standing by the railing, while Maurice remained on the cushioned sofa, hands tucked under the cushions as he tried to grasp the unwieldy shotgun.

All three of them froze at the sight of her. Paige Stevens was the first to recover. "I've seen you before. You were the woman in the restaurant. Who took my purse…"

"She's the investigator my daughter hired." Maurice swore. He'd finally managed to pull out the weapon Paige had hidden earlier and now he cradled it in both hands. "What in God's name are you doing here? Celia promised me she'd called you off."

"Well, I'm here now and you've got bigger problems on their way." Lindsay glanced at her watch, hoping they couldn't see how badly she was trembling. Nathan had been right. She posed no threat to a man holding a gun. All she could do was try to bluff her way out of the situation.

"I called the cops," she announced, trying to sound confident. "They'll be here any minute."

Maurice swore again, but Paige remained cool. "That's okay, we can still handle this. Maurice, you'll say your wife shot her first, then loaded the gun again and turned it on you. You wrestled the weapon from her hands and it accidentally discharged. Our plan will still work, but we have to act fast."

Audrey's face turned whiter with each word Paige uttered. Now she leaned heavily on the railing for support as she turned betrayed eyes toward the man she'd married.

"This can't be happening. Maurice, look at me."

But he wouldn't. Or couldn't. He tightened his grip on the shotgun as Paige continued to give him instructions.

"We have to stay calm," the redhead said. "We've got too much at stake not to follow through. All these months of planning have led to this. Don't be afraid, Maurice. You can do it."

"Months of planning?" Audrey sounded helplessly confused, but Lindsay wasn't.

"This started last August, didn't it?" she said. "Audrey the reason you don't remember shooting your husband is because you didn't. The whole scenario was staged. Maurice wounded himself, or possibly his lover, Paige Stevens, helped him with that little task."

As she talked, she noticed Nathan sneaking up from the opposite side of the building. He must have crept around back. God, he must be furious at her for landing them in this mess. She wished she could tell him to wait for the cops. The last thing she wanted was for him to get hurt, too.

He'd been right. She'd been crazy to think she could save Audrey. All she'd done was jeopardize herself, and Nathan, too, if he didn't run for cover.

"You slipped something into my coffee that morning," Audrey realized. "I thought it was strange that you'd made breakfast for me. I can't believe you put me through that nightmare. I thought I was crazy."

She started to move toward her husband, then stopped as he raised the shotgun.

Lindsay felt the blood rush from her head at the sight. It took all her strength to remain standing and to contain the screams she could feel building inside of her.

Meanwhile, Audrey was staring down her husband. "I don't even know you anymore. You're a monster."

"I didn't have a choice," he reiterated.

"Like hell you didn't," Lindsay responded.

Maurice reacted by swinging his gun up to his shoulder. First he aimed at his wife, then at her.

"Do it, Maurice," Paige urged.

Lindsay was trembling so badly now she could hardly keep standing. She flattened her palms against her legs. They were soaked with sweat.

Around her the world darkened. She wasn't outside anymore, but in a room. There was blood everywhere and her father was turning to her. He had a gun in his hands, too. He was lifting it. Pointing it at her.

A wild, terrible pain spread inside of her. Her father had been about to shoot her, that day. She'd known it then and she knew it now. Only Meg's sudden appearance in the room had stopped him.

"Daddy?" As Meg started to scream, their father had

taken the gun which he'd been pointing at Lindsay and had aimed it at his own head and squeezed the trigger.

Lindsay shut her eyes as tightly as she could. Logically she knew she was a grownup now, that this was a different time. But it didn't matter. Her mother was dead. She wanted to die, too.

Go ahead and shoot me. It's okay.

Then something thudded hard on the porch. Instinctively Lindsay turned in the direction of the sound just as Nathan hurled himself across the porch. He flung his arms around Maurice's legs and the man toppled like a bowling pin, the gun crushed between him and the porch floor.

And finally, finally, came the sound of a siren.

Lindsay's knees gave out and she sank to the ground. Nathan pried the gun out from under Maurice, then motioned at Paige to step up to the porch. When she looked as though she was going to run, he forestalled her with a dangerously hard voice. "You should know I'm a trained cop. I know how to use this gun, so I wouldn't put me to the test if I were you."

Silently Paige did as he asked. Nathan gestured for her to sit on the sofa next to Maurice, then, keeping the gun trained on them both, he settled back to wait for help.

"Are you okay?" he asked Audrey.

"I—I think so."

"Please check on Lindsay."

Audrey made her way slowly from the porch. She sank to the ground next to Lindsay and took her hand. Tears streamed so quickly from Lindsay's eyes she could hardly make out the older woman's features.

"Can I get you something?" Audrey asked gently.

She couldn't answer. Audrey placed an arm around her shoulders and it felt good.

"You saved my life," the woman said softly. "You were very brave."

She wasn't brave now. Lindsay didn't know what was wrong with her. Actually she did. She was having some sort of breakdown. She could not stand up and could not stop crying. What she really wanted was for Nathan to come and hold her. But she understood that he couldn't. Not until help had arrived.

THE SIRENS GREW LOUDER.

"Hang in there, Fox." Nathan wished he could go to her, but he didn't dare take his eyes off Maurice and Paige for a second. "Help is almost here," he added to encourage her.

They'd been in dangerous situations before, and he'd never seen her break down like this. There had to be something specific about this scenario that had got to her.

He was grateful that Audrey had gone to comfort her. The two women were kneeling on the ground, arms wrapped around one another. Soon shock was going to hit Audrey, and hard, but for now Lindsay's obvious distress was a distraction.

Noticing Maurice and Paige making eye contact, he pushed the shotgun between their faces. "You two are pretty good at ideas, aren't you? Don't get any new ones. I'm fed up, as it is."

In the daylight, with minimal makeup, Paige's age was more obvious. He turned to Maurice. "So how much do you know about this woman you think you love? Did she tell you about her past in New Hampshire? The older husband who died of 'digestive troubles.'"

Having witnessed Paige's diabolical mind in action, he was doubly suspicious about her past.

"Good thing the authorities didn't look too closely into your first husband's death, wasn't it?"

"Don't be ridiculous," she snapped, but he could almost smell her fear. Beside her Maurice looked grayer, smaller, older. Nathan could tell all the fight had gone out of him. Still, he didn't allow his vigilance to slacken for even an instant.

The wailing of sirens crescendoed as a marked police cruiser emerged from the woods. Two uniformed officers stepped out of the car, guns drawn. Only when they were firmly in control of the situation, and Paige and Maurice had both been cuffed, did Nathan go to Lindsay.

The younger of the two officers helped Audrey up from the ground, gently leading her to the cruiser in order to ask her questions.

That left Nathan with Lindsay. He folded her into his arms. "It's okay, sweetheart. You're okay."

He'd never imagined someone so strong could break down so completely. It broke his heart to see the tears flowing from her beautiful blue eyes. She looked completely lost and without hope.

"What's the point?" she finally whispered. "Maybe he should have shot me. That might be easier."

Nathan wasn't sure what she was talking about. But he could guess. "Your parents...were they shot?"

She nodded. "I was supposed to die, too."

Nathan was too confused to know what to say. He pressed one of her hands against his cheek. She was so cold. "There must have been a reason you didn't."

Slowly his words sank in and Lindsay nodded. "To help other people."

He thought about her work, how she gave her all to everything she did. "Yes, in part. But you deserve something, too. Maybe it's time you allow yourself happiness. Allow yourself love."

He pressed a kiss to her forehead, then to her cheek. Her skin was damp with salty tears. He pulled her face to his shirt and held her next to his aching heart and knew two things for certain.

She would never be easy to love. But he would always love her.

ANOTHER POLICE CAR AND an ambulance showed up half an hour after the authorities first appeared. While Lindsay and Audrey were being treated for shock, Nathan overheard the cops interviewing Maurice and Paige separately. With their plans exposed, Paige was suddenly playing innocent, claiming Maurice had orchestrated everything and describing, in detail, how he had set his wife up on that day in August.

Eventually both Maurice and Paige were arrested and driven away. Audrey called a neighbor who arrived quickly and offered to put her up for the night. Nathan and Lindsay drove to the police station to provide full statements. When they were finally finished it was late afternoon. Nathan gently helped Lindsay back into the gray rental car. He fastened the seat belt for her and covered her with both blankets. She was asleep before he'd reached the main highway.

On the road he called Nadine and asked her to open the office and get hold of Lindsay's sister. "Ask her to meet us at the office. We should be there by six."

Nadine was clearly dying to find out what had happened at the Burchards' lodge, but he promised to fill her and Meg in once they were home. He didn't want to disturb Lindsay's sleep with unnecessary conversation. She was totally flaked out and God knew she needed the rest.

It was almost six o'clock by the time he'd returned the car to the rental company. He and Lindsay took a cab to the office. Lindsay was still groggy and didn't feel like talking. She let him hold her hand, though, and he contented himself with that.

Nadine and Meg were both waiting when they walked in the door. He could tell they were shocked by Lindsay's appearance. She was still pale, her hair tousled and her eyes red and puffy. More than that, her indomitable spirit had been wounded.

Her receptionist and her sister flanked her, pushing Nathan gently out of the way. They settled her on the sofa in the reception area, and Nathan went to make coffee, only to discover Nadine already had a pot brewed.

"Food is on the way," Nadine said. "I've ordered Vietnamese hot soup and salad rolls."

"Good idea," he said, realizing that he and Lindsay hadn't eaten all day except for coffee at the police station and their early morning breakfast of juice and granola bars.

A delivery boy showed up soon after, and it turned out that Nadine had also ordered lemongrass chicken and lots of rice. Everyone shared the food, and even after Nathan and the others were full, Lindsay kept eating. She ate and ate, and had several cups of hot, black coffee.

Finally she smiled and looked like herself again. "I feel better," she announced as if she was surprised. Nathan was, too. After all she'd been through, he'd thought it would take more than one nap and a proper meal to revive her.

"So tell us what happened," Nadine urged.

"I've been so worried," Meg added.

"I forgot to cancel our Saturday lunch," Lindsay realized. "Meg, I'm sorry."

"Never mind that right now. I want to hear what you were up to. Nadine told me about the case, so I know that you and Nathan went out to the Catskills to make sure your clients were happily reconciled. I take it the reconciliation never happened?"

"Maurice had no intention of patching things up with his wife," Lindsay said. "He wanted to lure Audrey out to the country so he and his mistress could kill her."

"Good God, why?" Meg asked. "A simple divorce would give him his freedom."

"It was his wife's money he didn't want to be parted from." Lindsay frowned. "Nathan, do you remember what happened with that real estate deal?"

"Maurice sank all his money into what was going to be his biggest project ever. But the financing fell apart and Maurice had to pay back all his investors. It sounds like it cleaned him out."

"So he decides to kill his wife, the mother of his only child?" Meg shook her head sadly. "How terrible."

"The plan was deviously intricate," Lindsay continued. "He and Paige set Audrey up to take the blame months ago. Audrey was tricked into thinking she'd tried to kill Maurice last August."

"She didn't?" Nadine asked.

"No. Paige told the cops everything. She said Maurice slipped some of those fast-acting date-rape drugs in with Audrey's breakfast that morning. About twenty minutes later, when they were out in the garden, she became disoriented, then partly unconscious. When she came to she was so groggy and confused, she thought she'd had a psychotic episode."

"They also played with the clocks at the lodge," Nathan explained, "so it seemed like less time had passed than actually had."

Lindsay nodded. "Audrey thought she'd slept in that morning, but Maurice had adjusted all the inside clocks by one hour. He and Paige needed the extra time so the drugs would wear off before the cops arrived."

"The police didn't run a toxicology screen on Audrey?" Meg asked.

"They used a drug called Special K or ketamine. The substance doesn't show up in the bloodstream unless you specifically look for it," Nathan explained.

"I think I get it," Nadine said slowly. "If Audrey tried to kill Maurice once, why not a second time? So when *Maurice* shoots *her,* he can claim self-defense."

Nathan grinned. "I knew you had potential, Nadine. That's exactly right. And the plan would have worked if Lindsay hadn't risked her life to stop it."

As Meg and Nadine gasped, Lindsay scowled at him. "Did you have to say that?"

"Hey, I'm tired of nagging you. I want some help."

"Well, you'll get it from me," Meg spoke up quickly. "Lindsay, you're all the family I've got. Please be more careful in the future."

Her sister's words were clearly heartfelt and Lindsay had the grace to look chastised. "I will try, Meg," she promised. The sisters hugged, then Meg made Lindsay describe in detail what had happened.

Though Nathan was worried reliving the experience might be too much for Lindsay, it turned out to be cathartic. There were more tears, and more conversation, and eventually Nadine made herbal tea.

Around nine o'clock, Lindsay started yawning. Meg picked up on her sister's exhaustion right away.

"You need to rest, but no way are you spending the night by yourself. I'll bring Sadie over and we'll sleep in your living room."

Lindsay's gaze sought his and his stomach tightened. He knew how he felt about her, but he had no idea how she felt in return. Without breaking eye contact Lindsay finally said, "That's okay, Meg. I'll be with Nathan."

"I WOULDN'T HAVE MADE IT through this day without you."

Lindsay was standing in the shower at her apartment with Nathan, his strong arms around her waist as she lathered shampoo through his hair.

"You're stronger than you think. Yes, you would have." Nathan rubbed the loofah gently down her back, over her buttocks, then up again.

Shampoo streamed from his hair over both of their bodies. She clung to him, exhausted from the day, the hot shower and the lovemaking they'd shared as soon as they'd found themselves alone.

She'd thought she was too tired to do anything. But Nathan's soft touch and loving words had revived her.

"I know I'm strong. But Maurice would have shot me if you hadn't tackled him when you did."

"Okay. Maybe I deserve a little credit," he said modestly.

She laughed, then fell silent. He'd seen her stripped naked today, in more ways than one. She wasn't totally comfortable with how vulnerable that made her feel. Not yet. But she knew she could trust Nathan and that was a good start.

"Clean enough?" she asked. "I'm going to fall asleep on my feet if we don't get out of here soon."

Nathan turned off the water, then held her hand as she stepped out of the shower.

"I'm not an invalid."

"Just let me take care of you a little. It's been a hard day." He wrapped one towel around his waist, then used the other to dry her gently. She succumbed to his administrations because, frankly, it felt damn nice.

Finally they were in bed together, naked, her head on his chest, his arms holding her close. They were silent for a long while, but she could tell he wasn't sleeping. She couldn't stop the day's events from playing through her mind. She was so glad they'd prevented Maurice from hurting Audrey. Celia's father would end up in prison, but she would have her mother, at least, and that was a lot.

She thought about the way she'd collapsed when

Maurice turned that gun on her. She was used to being tough in demanding situations, but she'd fallen apart. Nathan had witnessed it all, her complete unraveling. If that hadn't scared him away, she didn't think anything could.

"What happened to my sister and me—you don't get over it. You just learn to live with it. And just when it starts to get easier, something happens and you feel like you're back to square one."

"Lindsay...what *did* happen? Are you ever going to be able to tell me?"

Suddenly Lindsay felt wide-awake. She sat up in bed and looked at him solemnly. "You know, I've never talked about this before. But you deserve the truth."

He sat up, too, arranged pillows behind her. "I take it this has something to do with why you changed your last name."

"You know about that?"

"Nadine saw some papers in the file cabinet. She told me when we were talking about *her* deception."

Lindsay nodded. "Well, it's true. Meg and I changed our last names when we left California. Yzereef is pretty distinctive and we wanted a fresh start."

She paused. Getting the words out was so damn hard. Maybe this would be easier if she just showed him one of the clippings.

She climbed out of bed and went to a shoe box at the back of her closet. After unfolding the yellowed paper, she passed it to Nathan.

NATHAN SWALLOWED, THEN STARTED reading out loud.

"In a hot and dusty California town, while most

families were huddled inside around air conditioners or splashing in backyard pools, two daughters witnessed their father's madness as he shot and killed first his wife, then himself."

Nathan stopped. He had to remind himself that he was reading about Lindsay, not some nameless, faceless victim. She was sitting on the bed beside him, and he took her hand in his. Maybe he shouldn't be reading this out loud.

"Keep going," she said.

He took a deep breath, then did as she'd asked. Midway through the article, the family was profiled. "Barry Yzereef was the local sheriff, his wife, Donna, taught science at the local school. Barry Yzereef was a hero from the Vietnam War, a winner of the Air Force Medal of Honor."

He lifted his head and looked at the medal in question. His stomach tightened, and so did his grip on Lindsay's hand.

Scrolling down the article, he saw the same photos of a young woman and a young man that were framed on Lindsay's bureau.

Though repelled and saddened, in equal measure, he couldn't stop reading. A thorough account of the crime followed and one sentence brought him to tears: "The daughters, ages eight and five, were splattered with blood but physically unharmed, according to the neighbor who was first on the scene."

Splattered with blood. The blood of their parents. Nathan remembered when Mary-Beth had been eight. She'd loved Care Bears and ponies and her biggest problem was dealing with her curly hair, which she hated. He tried to imagine her witnessing what Lindsay had witnessed.

It was inconceivable.

The final paragraphs of the article turned to analysis. "Why did this happen? A full answer will probably never be known, though coworkers had noted a change in Yzereef's behavior in the weeks prior to the tragedy. Depression, uncharacteristic anger, mumbling under his breath, may have been signals of a mental illness that were unfortunately dismissed. His experiences in the Vietnam War may have contributed to his breakdown."

Nathan placed the article on the bedside table. Lindsay had curled into a ball beside him, and he wrapped his body around hers. Outside the traffic noises continued unabated. Life always went on in New York City, no matter what sorrows occurred behind the brick faces and curtained windows of the apartment buildings and storefronts that lined the crowded streets.

Nathan couldn't think. His mind was numb. He supposed it was a form of shock.

He'd suspected he would find out something bad.

But he had never imagined this.

THE NEXT MORNING, LINDSAY sent Nathan out to get a paper while she made a pot of coffee. Considering all she'd been through yesterday, she felt surprisingly well and full of energy today.

Spending the night in Nathan's arms probably had a lot to do with that.

She'd just filled two mugs with coffee, when Nathan returned. He handed her the Sunday edition of the *Daily News*. The arrest of Maurice Burchard and Paige

Stevens had made the front page, and Fox Investigations was mentioned several times in the accompanying article.

"You are going to be flooded with clients after this," Nathan predicted.

"Don't you mean, *we?*" Lindsay asked hopefully.

"I thought you were opposed to mixing business with pleasure. I was on the verge of going back to the police department, you know."

She went quiet, knowing that she had to think about what would be best for Nathan, not just what she wanted. "Would that make you happy? To be a cop, again?"

"All I know for sure is that I want to make a difference."

"Well, you sure made a difference yesterday. You were a true hero. Just like your father. You risked your life and you saved Audrey *and* me."

Nathan grinned. "Well. When you put it that way. Which sounds better? Fisher and Fox? Or Fox and Fisher?"

"Fox and Fisher," she said, intending to argue the point forcefully. There was nothing more she wanted than to work with him by her side...but she *had* started the business.

Then she realized he'd been yanking her chain, just like that first time, in her office.

"You drive a tough bargain, sweetheart, but Fox and Fisher is fine by me. We are going to need new business cards and stationery, though."

"On Monday I'll get Nadine on that."

"Not to mention new signage for the building."

"Signage? That sounds permanent."

Nathan took her left hand and touched the fourth finger. "That's how I'm thinking. Permanent."

"Permanent. I like the sound of that."

Hard to believe she'd ever thought Nathan was anything but the perfect partner. She squeezed his hand, not wanting to ever let him go.

* * * * *

*Fox and Fisher Investigations is so busy,
Lindsay and Nathan need another investigator! Too
bad they have different people in mind. Lindsay is
backing her friend Kate Cooper while Nathan wants
to hire his buddy Jay Savage.*

*Find out who gets the job in
THE P.I. CONTEST by C. J. Carmichael,
available in February 2010.*

*Fan favorite Leslie Kelly is bringing her readers a
fantasy so scandalous,
we're calling it FORBIDDEN!*

*Look for
PLAY WITH ME
Available February 2010 from Harlequin® Blaze™.*

"AREN'T YOU GOING TO SAY 'Fly me' or at least 'Welcome Aboard'?"

Amanda Bauer didn't. The softly muttered word that actually came out of her mouth was a lot less welcoming. And had fewer letters. Four, to be exact.

The man shook his head and *tsked*. "Not exactly the friendly skies. Haven't caught the spirit yet this morning?"

"Make one more airline-slogan crack and you'll be walking to Chicago," she said.

He nodded once, then pushed his sunglasses onto the top of his tousled hair. The move revealed blue eyes that matched the sky above. And, yeah. They were twinkling. Damn it.

"Understood. Just, uh, promise me you'll say 'Coffee, tea or me' at least once, okay? Please?"

Amanda tried to glare, but that twinkle sucked the annoyance right out of her. She could only draw in a slow breath as he climbed into the plane. As she watched her passenger disappear into the small jet, she had to wonder about the trip she was about to take.

Coffee and tea they had, and he was welcome to them.

But her? Well, she'd never even considered making a move on a customer before. Talk about unprofessional.

And yet...

Something inside her suddenly wanted to take a chance, to be a little outrageous.

How long since she had done indecent things—or decent ones, for that matter—with a sexy man? Not since before they'd thrown all their energies into expanding Clear-Blue Air, at the very least. She hadn't had time for a lunch date, much less the kind of lust-fest she'd enjoyed in her younger years. The kind that lasted for entire weekends and involved not leaving a bed except to grab the kind of sensuous food that could be smeared onto—and eaten off—someone else's hot, naked, sweat-tinged body.

She closed her eyes, her hand clenching tight on the railing. Her heart fluttered in her chest and she tried to make herself move. But she couldn't—not climbing up, but not backing away, either. Not physically, and not in her head.

Was she really considering this? God, she hadn't even looked at the stranger's left hand to make sure he was available. She had no idea if he was actually attracted to her or just an irrepressible flirt. Yet something inside was telling her to take a shot with this man.

It was crazy. Something she'd never considered. Yet right now, at this moment, she was definitely considering it. If he was available...could she do it? Seduce a stranger. Have an anonymous fling, like something out of a blue movie on late-night cable?

She didn't know. All she knew was that the flight to Chicago was a short one so she had to decide quickly.

And as she put her foot on the bottom step and began to climb up, Amanda suddenly had to wonder if she was about to embark on the ride of her life.

Sold, bought, bargained for or bartered

He'll take his...

Bride on Approval

Whether there's a debt to be paid,
a will to be obeyed or a business
to be saved...she has no choice
but to say, "I do"!

PURE PRINCESS,
BARTERED BRIDE

by *Caitlin Crews*
#2894

Available February 2010!

LARGER-PRINT BOOKS!
GET 2 FREE LARGER-PRINT NOVELS PLUS
2 FREE GIFTS!

HARLEQUIN*

Super Romance

Exciting, emotional, unexpected!

HSRLP10

PREGNANT BRIDES

Inexperienced and expecting,
they're forced to marry!

Bestselling Harlequin Presents author

Lynne Graham

brings you the second story
in this exciting new trilogy:

RUTHLESS MAGNATE, CONVENIENT WIFE
#2892

Available February 2010

Also look for

GREEK TYCOON, INEXPERIENCED MISTRESS
#2900

Available March 2010

HP12892